Across to America

by

Richard Testrake

Dedicated to my wife Peggy, my daughter Lisa and my son Charles

Table of Contents

CHAPTER ONE

On board HMS Andromeda, Land's End bearing NNE, distance 2 leagues

Captain Tim Phillips winced as another trickle of icy spray found its way under the sail-cloth covering he had spread over his body. It was time for the morning watch to come on deck, and he had spent the night in this frigid winter weather in a deck chair some hands had put together for him. Two of his officers stood on the lee side of the quarterdeck, wondering if it would be wise to approach him at this time. Lieutenant Gould was first officer while Lieutenant Darby was second. The third, Mister Goodrich, was below having stood the midnight watch.

Gould was a perfectly good officer, but something of an old maid. He was curious why his captain felt it necessary to spend much of most nights on deck. Gould was privately concerned his captain was finding his officers lacking in their abilities. Perhaps he felt it necessary to check up on them.

Phillips did have a perfectly good bed in his sleeping cabin, or at least what was left of it. He had been given command of this post ship just recently, his mission being to carry a diplomat to the Spanish Province of Venezuela on the South American continent. Apparently, insurgents were making a bid for independence from the Regency government of Spain, and HM government wished to have a representative there to view the situation.

The diplomat, one Lord Forsythe, however proved to be a trial, in more than one way. First of all, his quarters, in view of the small size of this post ship, were in the place of the captain's normal sleeping cabin. This housed the envoy and his servant. Captain Phillips removed himself to the adjoining space which had been used as his office.

Secondly, Lord Forsythe proved to be a poor sailor. He had been sick since leaving Portsmouth, and had shown no signs of recovering. Only a thin temporary partition separated the two sleeping compartments. Whenever Phillips attempted to get some sleep in the tiny space he had left, he was kept awake by the sounds and aroma of a constantly retching man. No stranger to cold and wet surroundings, he had opted to spend much of the time in his deck chair, swathed in a boat cloak with an extra sail cloth cover.

Finally, there were some strange orders regarding Forsythe's mission. He had been given a packet with the seals of both the Admiralty and of the Foreign Office, with orders the seals were not to be broken until south of eighteen degrees north latitude in the presence of Forsythe personally.

Lord Forsythe was to be delivered to the port of Caracas or such other port the envoy might select. In the absence of the envoy, for any reason, the ship should be put about and returned to the nearest British port.

In the dim glow of the binnacle light he saw two, blue-coated men approaching his chair. One was Mister Harding, his sailing master, the other proved to be Doctor Baynes, the ship's surgeon. The doctor had been spending much of his time with his most important patient, Lord Forsythe, avoiding as much as possible the routine medical difficulties of the crew. He regarded his special patient to be the reason for his being on this ship and avoided the remainder of the ship's population as best he could. Fortunately, there was a man aboard Andromeda who had once served Phillip's father as a loblolly boy on his ship. This man was assigned to the same position to serve the good doctor and was able to furnish much of the routine care the men expected.

Phillips did not deem that patient's comfort and well-being to be the most important of his own concerns. At the moment, Andromeda's exact position in relation to nearby Land's End was, and he spoke to Harding first.

Harding had had leadsmen in the main chains all night, swinging the heavy lead weight on its line out ahead and measuring the depth by means of pieces of differing pieces of material knotted into the line a fathom apart. The leadsman was trained to identify each such piece using just the sense of touch in the dark, thus being capable of instantly calling out the depth. In addition to measuring the depth of the waters, a recess on the lead weight could be charged with tallow, which could collect samples of the bottom sediment...

From his charts and own personal knowledge, Harding was able to determine with fair accuracy the ship's likely location, just by the depth and the make-up of the sea bottom.

The nightlong downpour of frigid rain had prevented any sight of land, but Harding reported the ship had fifteen fathoms under its keel and he estimated land to be two leagues to the NNE.

Since Harding seemed to be presently satisfied as to their current relative safety, Phillips turned to the doctor.

The surgeon, not a career ship's doctor, had been produced by the Foreign Office specifically to tend to the medical needs of Lord Forsythe. The envoy, on land a perfectly healthy individual, readily admitted his absolute helplessness at sea.

Doctor Baynes had been furnished a warrant as Ship's Surgeon and found himself on the books with the task of administering not only to the envoy, but the entire ship's crew. At least, that was the Royal Navy's view. The doctor himself had the understanding that this voyage was to be a vacation with the only duty of tending to the envoy's health. The Royal Navy's opinion that he was also to see to the health of the ship's crew was of no concern of his,

He had not much idea of his real place in the ship's hierarchy, considering himself one of the ranking members of the crew, perhaps subordinate only to the captain.

Phillips had found himself explaining matters to his own first officer who had taken offense at the doctor giving him orders as to his duty. It seemed the good doctor had deemed the pitching and rolling of the ship injurious to the health of his patient and had ordered Lieutenant Gould to reduce the ship's motion. Harsh words had resulted, and Captain Phillips had found himself attempting to pacify matters.

The good doctor had difficulty understanding his actual status aboard ship was that of a relatively junior warrant officer rather than equivalent or superior to a commissioned officer like the ship's lieutenants. Recognizing the doctor to be a very knowledgeable physician rather than one of the usual inept drunks they were often given to tend to the men's health, he was inclined to allow affronts to his dignity to pass by unchallenged.

Baynes was on deck now with the sailing master and as soon as Mister Harding finished his report, stepped up to deliver the latest prognosis. He felt Lord Forsythe would be all the better if he could be brought up on deck, if only for a few moments, and wondered if the weather would be conducive to that visit.

A questioning look from Phillips, elicited that opinion from Harding; his view being the weather would moderate later in the day, with the slight chance of a little sun. Phillips by now, regarded Harding as a weather prophet, and assured the doctor he could count on fair weather later that day.

Phillips was not anxiously awaiting the appearance of Lord Forsythe on deck. He happened to be in a delicate position. Last year, he had been tasked to attempt to locate the missing wife of Forsythe's. She had been taken by Moorish pirates from a transport taking her home to deliver her unborn child in the peace and comfort of their home.

Instead, she found herself violently abused by these rovers and sold into slavery to the local strongman of an island off the coast of Cyprus. Along the way, her fetus had aborted and she was then newly impregnated by the attentions of some pirate. Her new owner, assuming he was the father of the child born of this coupling, treated the infant with some parental attention, although similar attention was not afforded the mother-to-be. The mother was just another slave, suffering the kicks and blows of the other concubines and wives.

After some searching and an inordinate amount of good fortune, her location had been discovered and Captain Phillips led a party ashore to rescue the woman. Lady Forsythe, believing, with good reason, she would be regarded with distain by her peers back in Britain and her child considered a bastard, initially refused to return, theorizing her child might have a better chance of a life in these surroundings, with this powerful father.

Phillips, believing it his duty to return Lady Forsythe, had compelled her return, later inventing the story her child was her husband's. The script being, she had merely been the slave of the strongman's wives, and had not suffered any attentions by him. Her husband's unborn child had never been aborted and here was the result.

After the woman was reunited with her husband and family, there was much excitement in the press and some demand for Phillips to come forth and recount his exploits.

The true nature of Lady Forsythe's sufferings were known to only a very few people high in the Admiralty, and it was agreed the best course would be to keep

Captain Phillips away from Britain until the furor had died. It was feared an enterprising reporter might somehow dig out the prurient details and ruin innocent lives.

Accordingly, Phillips was promoted to the rank of post captain and given the mission to take an envoy to South America. This should keep him away from Britain for a lengthy period, during which time the press would surely find some other matter with which to excite themselves. Unfortunately, at the last minute, the envoy that had long been scheduled to make the voyage, suffered an accident involving his overturned coach and it was necessary to replace him.

The official making that decision was not aware of the situation concerning Lord Forsythe's family and at the very last moment, Forsythe appeared on Andromeda's deck with his effects, as the newly designated envoy. Believing another change at the last moment could be suspicious, it was decided to go with this plan. Phillips was counselled to keep his distance from the envoy and to decline to elaborate on Lady Forsythe's ordeal.

Phillips had a certain amount of anxiety at first, certain Forsythe would be able to guess the true events and subject him to questioning that he was not certain he could answer.

To his relief however, Forsythe became violently ill while being pulled out to Andromeda in choppy waters of the harbor, and immediately asked to be taken to his quarters.

Apparently though, now was the time of reckoning. To evade the envoy as long as possible, the captain was tempted to go forward and inspect the starboard cat-head, or some other duty requiring intense concentration, but common civility had him remain aft.

CHAPTER TWO

It was a pale and weakened man helped to the quarterdeck by his servant and Doctor Baynes. Phillips had vacated the deck chair and Lord Forsythe was helped into it. The servant spread a fur robe over the official and Forsythe pronounced himself superbly comfortable.

He began by apologizing profusely for his absence thus far because of his *mal de mer* and thanking his captain for the rescue of his wife and son from the clutches of the pirates.

"Captain Phillips, had it not been for your action, my family would have suffered a dreadful fate. I owe you much, sir!"

Phillips responded, assuring the envoy any naval officer would have done as much, probably a good bit faster.

Forsythe was not convinced for a moment. "Sir, it was you that saved the life of my son and wife, and no one can convince me differently. I tell you, I am not without influence at Court, and I made it known to the Crown that you should be given proper recognition. However, it seemed you were away on the other side of the world and could not be produced."

Captain Phillips escaped with the declaration he must go forward at this time to inspect the foremast backstay. In the following days, it became necessary for the captain to spend much of the time whenever the envoy was on deck inspecting the various elements of the standing and running rigging. The deck officers were given orders to approach when conversation between captain and passenger became intense and request Phillip's guidance upon some point.

Andromeda continued on course. The weather did improve to some extent in the coming days. Early in the afternoon watch one day, the sails of an approaching convoy were seen. Too far away for signals to be read, Phillips ordered the course altered a few points in order to make his manners with its escort.

Closing in, it became evident there was some disarray. As soon as signals from the leading escort frigate could be read, she was revealed her to be HMS Alceste, 38 guns, Captain Murray commanding. The signal, repeated from HMS Stately, further indicated the convoy was under attack by the enemy and assistance was required.

With the Marine drummer hammering away, Andromeda cleared for action. All partitions were knocked down, including the envoy's quarters. Lord Forsythe appeared on the quarterdeck with a wicked looking epee in his hand, and his manservant clutching an ornate fowling piece. He approached Captain Phillips and informed him that he was at his service.

"My man informs me pirates are in the vicinity. Where would you like me posted, Captain?"

Captain Phillips had to gather his thoughts. "Milord, I suspect our enemy will more likely be French privateers out to try to make off with a ship from that convoy we are approaching. If you wish to look through my glass, you will see the flock scattering."

The convoy was indeed breaking up. There now appeared to be three escorts for about a forty ship convoy. One was a stodgy old 64. Another was the Alceste and finally a non-rated brig. There appeared to be two predators after the convoy. One a sleek schooner, probably packed with men and a brig. Both were agile craft and dangerous indeed to any lightly armed merchantman they came up against.

The two larger escorts would have a difficult time dealing with the enemy privateers. Philips explained to Forsythe the problem. "Milord, a consortium of French businessmen will purchase a fast ship, pack it full of men and give it a few guns for armament and a letter of marque. These men will not be paid. They will be fighting for shares in the value of any prize they take, so there isn't all that much expense involved."

"I think we have two privateers to contend with today. Their plan doubtless is to frighten the individual ship masters of the convoy and scatter them. At that point, they will attempt to close a ship that has separated from the convoy, swarm her with masses of boarders and sail her off before the escorts can interfere. They will rightly assume the escorts will be too busy with getting the convoy back into order to pursue them."

"But Captain Phillips, I understand there are three powerful King's ships protecting the convoy. Surely they can handle a pair of poorly armed small craft?"

"Lord Forsythe, you would indeed think so. However, the difficulty arises in the escorts themselves. We have a powerful 64 gun ship-of-the line, capable of handling almost any French National ship now at sea. However, she is old and slow, unable to maneuver with the predators. Then there is the frigate which is also a most capable ship with her eighteen pounder long guns and thirty two pounder carronades. But, she also is not nearly as agile as the privateers, and a capable captain and crew on one of those could give the frigate a difficult time."

"The escort brig should be a capable enough craft, but it will not like coming up against one of the privateers by itself. Each of them probably have many more men than the escort does, and if the brig cannot get in some severe blows before closing, there is the danger of the escort herself being taken. It would be well to remember, these escorts have, perhaps, forty merchantmen to protect. When they scatter, the escorts have the devil's own time protecting them."

"I intend to try to close one of these vessels. With our efforts, along with those of the escorts, I hope to repel the attack. Perhaps if we are fortunate, we may indeed be able to take one of them, or possibly cause some important damage. If we can at least disable one, the rest of us should be able to negate the other."

"If you wish, Milord, you are welcome to go up on the mizzen top and engage any close targets with your fowling piece, should we close."

17

Lord Forsythe glanced up at the little platform far above the deck and slowly shook his head. "I am afraid I have a poor head for heights, Captain. Perhaps I should remain here on deck."

"You would indeed be welcome to remain here, Milord. However, for the record, let it be said I have asked you to go below for safety. There may be shot flying soon, and I would not want it said that I prevented you from going to a place of safety."

CHAPTER THREE

Matters were more complex than the captain had related to Lord Forsythe. He had not had occasion to obtain his usual private stock of powder and shot for training his gun crews. Many of the ranking officials in the hierarchy of the Royal Navy believed it was not necessary to practice live fire. After all, all that needed done was to place your ship up against the enemy, fire a couple of broadsides into her at close pistol shot range and board her in the smoke.

With senior officials of the Admiralty regarding actual firing of the guns in practice to be almost pointless, there were strict limits to the use of the ammunition. Only a small fraction of the issue charges were allowed to be expended in the first six months of the voyage, unless fired into a legitimate military or naval target.

At any rate, most of the gunnery practice of the ship's crew had been just the daily practice of running the guns up to the ports, simulating firing, then hauling them back to simulate loading. Phillips had ordered his officers to question members of the crew to find any long-service hands who may have had training from another captain in the past.

A dozen men turned up claiming to have served under men whom Phillips knew believed in proper training at firing guns accurately from a distance. These men were stationed at the two forward guns on the ship. Since there were insufficient gun crew to serve the guns of both sides at the same time, the crewmen of a particular gun would also serve the corresponding gun on the opposite side of the ship in case there was need.

While the ship approached the convoy, the gunner went around the ship with the captain, explaining to the gun crews, what was about to happen. The crew was not entirely ignorant of their expected duties. They had all spent at least an hour every day, sometimes much more, practicing simulated gun drill. But, Phillips knew, it would not be until the men heard the great guns crashing and men screaming from their horrible wounds that they could hope to understand what they would be facing

With all guns loaded and the tompions that prevented spray from entering the gun's bores removed, the midshipmen went down the row of guns, inspecting the gun locks for sharp flints and dry priming powder.

Approaching the convoy, Phillips had time to examine the current situation. HMS Stately, a perfectly respectable line-of-battle ship, was up forward on the windward van. Many of the merchants had clustered around her. The frigate was also to windward, but farther back the convoy was steadily shredding, with individual masters going in their own way.

The escort brig, Ferret, was in the rear attempting to protect a pair of merchants that had run aboard each other in panic and were now trying to extricate themselves.

The privateer brig, about the same size as her opponent, was closing in on the escort, perhaps in bluff, possibly with the view of swarming her with boarders, while giving the schooner free access to others ahead who might not be reached in time by the other two escorts.

Leaving the escort brig to her own devices for now, Phillips bulled ahead through the flock of merchants to the area where the schooner seemed to be headed. Judging he had a few minutes before the engagement commenced, he went forward to the pair of forward starboard guns he had staffed with his best people. He informed the crews he would be engaging to starboard for now, but the men must be prepared to rush across the deck to the opposite guns in case of need. He asked if any had questions or concerns.

A grizzled man with a pigtail down his back shifted his quid and answered. "Sir, if you please, we know some of the other gun crews are lubbers, that couldn't hit the Victory if she was lashed to our side, but we can do the job. Just tell us what you want from us."

The man's name came then to Phillips. The seaman had served with him on a previous voyage to the Baltic.

"Fletcher, I need to disable one or the other of those privateers, preferably both. I will tell you this now, the first crew to knock away an important spar will have a monumental drunk from me. The winner would take over my quarters and I will see you have all the grog you can handle."

"In addition, we need another gunner's mate. The captain of the gun that knocks away that spar will instantly be promoted to gunner's mate. Now, if either of you gun captains see a clear shot that may result in a good hit, you have my permission to fire. Are we understood?"

21

There was a buzz among the men as he went back aft. The enemy schooner was closing on a pair of ship rigged traders. She was apparently trying to persuade them to scatter, but Phillips was thinking she might have left it too late. Realizing her danger from the British warship, the schooner fired her port broadside into one of the merchants, perhaps trying to cripple her. With only two guns on that side, the attempt failed and the schooner turned to flee.

Mister Harding, handling the ship while Phillips kept his eye on the situation, turned with her. As Andromeda wheeled around, for a moment her broadside was trained on the enemy. Phillips had raised his arm and was readying himself to drop it as a signal, when he saw Fletcher behind his gun, sighting down the barrel and urging men with crows to lever it around a bit more. Phillips dropped his arm, and all of the other guns fired, except for Fletcher's. Phillips saw several balls smash into the lightly built hull of the enemy but nothing vital was carried away.

It was then Fletcher pulled the lanyard of his gun. A second after the gun recoiled savagely to the rear, Phillips saw the schooner's foremast lean a bit. Through his glass, Phillips could see the splintered notch on the mast and a split beginning to travel up it. As the schooner continued its turn, the split travelled further up the mast then suddenly the whole foremast came crashing down in a tangled mess of sailcloth and rigging.

As Andromeda passed her, she fired the few guns that had been reloaded into the schooner without effect, then coming around to the assistance of the escort brig, which was locked in combat with the other privateer.

Closing, a mass of humanity was struggling aboard Ferret, with boarders from the enemy outnumbering Ferret's crew.

Stately was bulling her way through the convoy with signal flags streaming, turning aside for no one, while HMS Alceste was acting as a sheep dog, attempting to get the flock back together again. As Andromeda closed on the combatants, the privateer's boarders were seen deserting Ferret's decks to scramble back aboard their own.

To no avail; Andromeda surged up to the small brig and fired her broadside into her from close pistol shot range. Most shots hit, but the privateer cut herself away from the trailing wreckage and tried sailing away. All guns were now ordered re-loaded with grape, and this load was fired into the enemy at long musket range.

Dozens of the swarming boarding crew were smashed to the deck, with gallons of blood spilling out of the scuppers, and then Stately was there. She proceeded to show the nippers how it was done. The privateer had managed to get away from Ferret, but Stately, with a good amount of way on her, came right up alongside and fired her full broadside into the little brig.

Afterward, everyone said that privateer captain was a fool for not hauling down his flag when he saw Stately approach. After Stately's massive discharge at close range, closely following Andromeda's broadside, the enemy ceased being an armed, sea-going vessel and instead was transformed into a mass of floating firewood.

Ship's boats and surgeons were kept busy the rest of the day. The boats searching out the few survivors of the smashed brig and ferrying the injured to whatever ships in the convoy with surgeons aboard. Half of Ferret's crew were dead or wounded, including her captain and the single first officer.

CHAPTER FOUR

A pair of officers and some seamen from Stately were brought aboard Ferret to re-inforce her crew. Phillips suspected some of Stately's midshipmen were about to be appointed acting lieutenants in lieu of the transferred officers. There were some wry looks among his own mids at the lost opportunity, but Phillips well knew some of these would have their chance before long.

Now it became the convoy's turn to furnish men to the warships. Officers with boarding crews went onto every ship in the convoy and determined whether any of the merchantmen could spare any people.

Of course many ships had aboard only the barest minimum of crew needed to make sail, but a few ships did have an adequate crew and these were the ones penalized. Naval crews were sent to the ships damaged in the action to assist in repairs. Besides the needs of Ferret, men were needed to man the crippled schooner which was snapped up by Alceste after the action.

She would furnish the only prize money available for the action since the destruction of the enemy brig eliminated any profit from her. There were some harsh words spoken about Stately's treatment of the privateer brig. Some felt Andromeda could have easily finished the task herself with the bonus of having an intact hull to sell afterward.

Captain Phillips saw some wondering looks from the men and was perplexed until he recalled his promise to the gun crews. With hands swarming around the ship, each bent on his own mission, he called over a carpenter's mate. Finding the first officer had assigned the petty officer and his crew the task of replacing a section of splintered deck an enemy shot had plowed up, Phillips judged this repair to be mainly cosmetic and not immediately necessary. Speaking first to Mister Gould, he ordered the petty officer to put a crew of men to work putting his quarters, along with that of the envoy's back together again. Before the action, all partitions had been knocked down and struck below to allow free access to the guns and to minimize injuries from flying splinters.

Now the envoy's gear was being brought up from below. Phillips ordered Mister Gould to belay the furnishing of his own quarters until later, but added he would like it if a five gallon cask of his own personal spirits were brought up. These spirits were the remnants of a supply purchased in Cape Colony in Southern Africa on a previous voyage. At the time, Phillips had thought the ship might run out of rum if she stayed out much longer so had purchased a supply of locally distilled spirits.

In the end, the liquor was not needed and Phillips had taking to using the potent liquor himself on occasion. When necessary work on the ship showed signs of completion, he spoke to the Royal Marine lieutenant assigned to the ship.

"Mister Watkins, who would you expect to be your steadiest Royal Marine, one who perhaps is not overly tempted by drink?"

Watkins though a moment. "You may be thinking of Private Larson. While he does take his ration of grog every day, I have never seen him incapacitated."

"Well sir, would you pass the word for Private Larson? While you are at it, you might do the same for Seaman Fletcher."

Larson and Fletcher both came at the run, Fletcher with a fair idea of what was involved. Phillips gave both the plan. "My sleeping quarters are now put together, but are still empty of furnishings. Private Larson, I promised the gun crews I would reward the gun crew that crippled the enemy schooner with a good drunk. I saw Seaman Fletcher here bring down her foremast and his gun crew wins the prize. I also believe the neighboring gun assisted, so these men will also share."

"I am allowing these men the use of my quarters tonight where they will have as much spirits as they can handle. Private Larson, you have been reported to me by your officer as a steady man. You will be provided a ladle with which to issue the liquor into each man's piggin."

"Every man may have as much spirits as he can handle, but he must not drink too rapidly. Every time the ship's bell is struck, at the end of every glass at the ship's binnacle, each man may receive one ladle of drink, then must wait until the next glass. You will not drink, Private Larson. Instead, you will be paid five shillings for this task and receive an extra tot of grog tomorrow.

Seaman Fletcher, you are this moment rated as Gunner's Mate. As such you will keep control of your men and prevent them from harming each other or the ship. One of Private Larson's mates will remain outside the closed door in case you need any assistance. If we are clear Petty Officer Fletcher, you may leave now to bring your mates aft, and the party will begin. It will end when I say it will."

The grim faced Lieutenant Gould was plainly disapproving when he learned of the party. He sourly wondered aloud what their envoy was going to think of a drunken orgy being held next to his own quarters.

"That is a very good question Mister Gould. However, Lord Forsythe will not mind sleeping elsewhere this night. Would you locate Mister Goodrich now and both of you see me when he is located?"

In due course, Gould and Goodrich reported to their captain on the quarterdeck. "I assume Mister Gould has informed you of the entertainment I am giving my gun crews tonight in my quarters, Mister Goodrich. I will be spending the night on deck as I often do, but there is the problem of Lord Forsythe. He may dislike spending the night next to a party of drunken sailors. I wonder if I could implore you to offer him the hospitality of your berth tonight. Would you be willing to spend the evening in the gunroom?"

Mister Goodrich, a midshipman himself until very recently and well familiar with gunrooms, was fatalistic and accepted the suggestion without demur. Mister Gould was another matter. Having held his commission nearly twenty years, he was well aware of his rights. One of those rights was his charge over the wardroom, where the officers ate and lived. It would have been more diplomatic had Phillips asked him first.

Phillips, having dealt with recalcitrant first lieutenants before, had made up his mind he would not defer to this officer. He was the captain of the ship and the other officers would just need to adapt.

CHAPTER FIVE

With matters settled, he next approached Lord Forsythe, now ensconced in Phillips own deck chair on the quarterdeck. The ship had travelled south enough to begin getting some pleasant temperatures, pleasant enough that is, if one was wearing a decent cloak.

He explained the situation with his gun crews and the party he was giving them for knocking down that schooner's mast. He said, "I fear they will become boisterous as the evening wears on and may become tiresome. I wonder if I can beg you to spend the night in a spare cabin in the wardroom. It is tiny, but I am sure it will be more comfortable than your present quarters with an orgy going on next door."

Forsythe assured him not to have any concerns. "Turnabout is fair play, Captain. I am told it is many a night you have slept on deck to escape my vile retching. This is the very least I can do."

The prize schooner had been left behind, with men and materials necessary to rig a jury foremast. Captain Moore in Stately, with more men under his command, assigned crew from his own ship to man her. There was grumbling aboard Andromeda, some of the newer men having a dim understanding of prize procedures, imagining Stately was trying to 'steal' the prize, while their own efforts had caused her capture.

Overhearing some bitter debate from a nearby work party, Phillips called over the watch officer and asked him to bring a delegation of these men to the quarterdeck. Lieutenant Darby spoke with Midshipman Otis who was supervising the work party, and soon the apprehensive seamen were standing before their captain on the quarterdeck.

"Men, you and the others in the crew have made me proud today. Your efforts have caused the enemy to surrender a fine schooner to us. When she is sold, all of us will share in the money she brings. Are there any questions?"

A rugged-looking man stepped forward. He was one of a group of 'Quota Men' that had been originally sent to the ship from their home county as men regarded by the county officials as people that could well be done without.

Often free with his fists, Landsman Willis was one hand with whom Phillips thought he might have to amend his own rule about punishment. Several of his officers felt Willis would be the better if he were triced up and given a dozen lashes now and again.

Willis knuckled his forehead, then ruined the effect by sneering, "Sir, we took the ship, now Stately takes it away from us. What about that, then?"

"Willis, Stately did not take her away from us. Captain Moore as senior officer decided his ship, with its larger crew, was better prepared to man and repair her. After making port, she will enter prize court proceedings, and will be sold with the money divided up between the crews of all King's ships in sight of the action. That is the rule."

Phillips walked away from the group, not wishing to debate this lout any longer. Approaching Otis, he asked if the mid had had much trouble with Willis. The mid answered, "He always has that sneer on his face, and often ignores me when I speak to him. Yesterday he told me his old granny was a better officer than I would ever be."

Phillips nodded. "Mister Otis, if that hand gives you or any other petty officer disrespect again, you will write his name down for captain's mast and give it to Lieutenant Gould. I have tried to be easy with the hands, but I see that some are getting the wrong ideas. Things will change."

Next morning, the first officer approached Phillips on the quarterdeck and lifted his hat in salute. "Sir, I have a man on report for punishment. Midshipman Otis tells me you had asked him to write him up."

"Yes, I did, Mister Gould. I believe the man in question is Landsman Willis?"

"Sir!"

"Very well. I spoke to Willis yesterday. I regarded his demeanor as lacking in respect. Mister Otis tells me he is frequently insolent with him. I ordered him to put the man on report on the next occasion. Now, what are we to hear about Landsman Willis?"

"Sir, Bosun's Mate Anderson, in the hearing of Midshipman Otis, ordered Landsman Willis to coil down the main topmast staysail halyard. Willis advised Anderson to get stuffed. When Otis then ordered Willis to do what he was told, Willis informed the mid he was nothing but a boil on the captain's ass, begging your pardon, sir. He refused to obey and Otis called Mister Darby who had the watch. Willis, who was probably under the influence of his evening grog ration, was insolent to Darby, and the man placed in restraints and put below."

Phillips glanced out at the convoy and then up at his sails. The wind was light at the time, out of the WNW and the convoy was on the port tack. With no immediate concerns at hand he thought he might as well get the problem taken care of.

Telling Gould he was about to hold captain's mast, and all customers should be presented, he went below to put on his good coat and hat. The gold buttons and lace flashing in the sun, he went back up on deck. The men off watch had been summoned up from below, and a party of men were securing a hatch cover upright to the mizzen. The Marine sergeant with a pair of men led the prisoner up to their captain, crashing to a halt, with Sergeant Wolfe reporting, "Prisn'er and escort present and correct, Sir!"

Phillips noted Landsman Willis had lost his sneer. He seemed almost concerned about his situation. The captain suspected some of his mates had been telling him stories of the punishments that could be imposed upon him.

Captain Phillips started, "Mister Otis, would you please tell us of the charges placed against Landsman Willis?"

Willis stood, clad in the best uniform available in the gunroom, reciting the misdeeds of the culprit.

Phillips, noting the absence of one report wondered. "Mister Otis, it was mentioned to me that you were an object of comparison. I heard that Landsman Otis compared you to a boil on my ass. Could this be true?"

His face red, the lad stammered he could not possibly say that to his captain.

"Very well, Mister Otis. We will drop that for now. It well might prove embarrassing to have that entered in the log. Let us move on. Have we any witnesses to our Landsman's musings? Bosun's Mate Anderson, perhaps?"

"Sir", uttered Anderson, "I don't rightly know what that word is you said."

"Well, what did you see or hear that may concern us, today?"

Anderson spoke up then, informing all of Willis' refusal to coil down the halyard as ordered and a litany of other offenses, including the reference to the captain's boil.

When Anderson finished, Phillips ruled he would not consider Willis' 'boil' statement in his ruling since it had not been mentioned in the charges. However, he cautioned, charges could still be preferred and the matter could be brought up at another time.

Now Phillips asked if anyone had anything to say for the man. This was normally the time when a supervisor would ask leniency for the defendant, giving some type of explanation for his action.

At first nobody stepped forward. Finally Midshipman Otis stepped forward as the silence mounted. "Sir", the mid uttered, "Landsman Willis always rolls his hammock in a seamanlike manner!"

There were several muffle guffaws at that, and a smirk from Willis. Phillips looked grave and announced this had no bearing on the case. Turning to Willis, he asked, "Landsman Willis, have you anything to say for yourself?" There was silence while Willis shuffled his feet, started to open his mouth, then remained silent. Captain Phillips let the silence mount for a few minutes the stated, "Sentenced to twelve lashes and forfeiture of all grog and tobacco for the next week. Doctor, do your duty!"

It was necessary for the ship's surgeon to declare the prisoner fit to stand for his punishment, but there was a problem. All the other ships officers and warrants were present, but Doctor Baynes was not among them.

Phillips realized that Baynes had still not become aware of all the ship's customs and rules and was willing to accommodate the man as much as possible. Further, his patient had kept him up most every night since the beginning of the voyage. Now however, Lord Forsythe was beginning to get his sea legs, and the nightly sickness had almost vanished, allowing Baynes to finally get some rest.

Regardless, his presence was required on the quarterdeck, and Otis was ordered to go below and fetch the good doctor immediately.

The hands stood there, chewing their quids and murmuring as the wait became longer. Finally Baynes appeared with the harried mid almost pushing the doctor up the ladder.

The doctor was outraged when he learned the reason for his summons. He stated, at Phillip's question, "Yes, I heard the call, but as a doctor I am not at the beck and call of any jumped-up sailor. Further, these proceedings have nothing to do with me."

With that, the doctor turned his back and began going down the ladder to the wardroom. Phillips goggled at this effrontery then turned to the Marine officer standing near him.

"Mister Watkins, you will favor me by having Baynes brought back up. You may wish to have a few of your Marines assist you."

With a shout to Sergeant Wolfe who was standing close by, Lieutenant Watkins repeated the captain's orders. A file of Royal Marines rushed below, and soon re-appeared, with the doctor's elbows firmly grasped by a pair of burly Marines.

Phillips almost laughed at the enraged, red-faced doctor, but held himself in check. Now was not the time to further inflame passions.

Phillips addressed Baynes, still in the firm grasp of the Marines. "Doctor Baynes, I will not require you to tell me what you meant by the remark you mentioned about 'jumped-up' sailors. I do hope you were not referring to me. As it happens, you do have a place in these proceedings. Namely, you are required, as ship's doctor, to pass judgment on Landsman Willis' health. We must know whether his health at this moment is such to withstand a dozen lashes of the cat o' nine tails."

The still furious Baynes lashed out himself. "You forced me up for this, you nincompoop? I'll have you know I will bring charges against you when I next see a magistrate. I am Lord Forsythe's physician. I have nothing to do with your shipboard brutality."

Captain Phillips considered. "Doctor, you seem to still have the wrong impression of your standing aboard. At the moment, you are not an imposing Harley Street physician. Instead, when you accepted the warrant the Sick and Hurt Board gave you before you came on the ship, you became a warrant officer of the Royal Navy, subject to the orders of all officers senior to you. Yes, you are Lord Forsythe's physician, but you are also physician to every member of this ship's crew."

"One of your duties is to examine defaulters before they come up for punishment. Should you refuse, you may be charged with mutiny."

Baynes sneered at the captain. "And what are you going to do to me if I refuse? Whip me also? I tell you, I am a gentleman and must not be threatened in this manner."

Phillips sighed. "Yes Doctor, you are a gentleman and holder of a Navy Warrant. You will not be triced up and lashed. However, I am charging you with mutiny at this time. You will be taken below, where you will remain confined in your cabin until such time as I can turn you over to higher authority. You will stand trial at court martial and suffer whatever sentence that may be imposed upon you. You may well hang, Doctor Baynes."

As the Marines began to hustle the doctor below, Lord Forsythe, who had been a silent witness to the events, spoke up. "Captain Phillips, I wonder if I may have a few words with the doctor?"

"You may indeed Milord. However, time is fleeting, and we have another matter to dispense with."

Phillips called his ship's officers as well as the sailing master over and ordered them to individually examine Landsman Willis and express their opinions on his ability to stand punishment, because of the refusal of the ship's doctor.

All officers stated after a brief glance at the prisoner they could see no reason that Willis could not withstand punishment.

Phillips addressed the bosun. "Very well, do your duty!"

The prisoner was tied to the upright grating, his face toward the mast and a leather apron strapped to his lower back to protect the kidney area. Then a petty officer stood behind the victim with a cat-o'-nine tails in his hands. The lash had been made specifically for this task and would be discarded overboard as soon as the punishment had been inflicted.

The Marine drummer stood nearby and began to slowly beat his instrument. At Phillip's nod and order. "Do your duty" the bosun's mate drew his arm back and struck Willis' back with full force, leaving nine red stripes where the lash had landed. Willis winced but made no other expression of pain. The other eleven lashes were laid on. The victim made not a sound during the punishment. At the end of the dozen, the petty officer backed away, and said, "Punishment inflicted, Sir."

Willis was unstrapped from the grating and a bucket of seawater was thrown over his now bloody back. This time he did let out a howl as the salt water burned his wounds.

Lord Forsythe, who had been below during much of the punishment, approached and reported, "Sir, Doctor Baynes says he is most sorry for his actions and wished to express his apologies. He assures me he had no idea of his role in the ship and thought he was just to tend to me. Doctor Baynes told me there will be no further instances of disobedience."

CHAPTER SIX

In due course, Doctor Baynes approached Captain Phillips on the quarterdeck and expressed his apologies personally. On his part, Phillips assured the doctor that he himself had over-reacted and offered his own. Fortunately the log had not yet been brought up to date, so the matter could be forgotten. The doctor explained he had not been thoroughly briefed concerning his duties.

His London practice had become very tiring for him and a friend employed at the Foreign Office informed him of this position. He understood he would be the personal physician of an important envoy to South America, and had fancied the voyage as something of a vacation. He had heard something of a Navy Warrant but that had little meaning to him and escaped his memory.

Back on Harley Street, he had been something of an important person and he assumed this would be the situation here. When he began receiving orders from all and sundry, he was sure he was being practiced upon.

Days later, the convoy had now gone as far south as it needed and was now to sail due west to the Windward Islands. HMS Andromeda would be leaving the convoy to continue on its course to its destination a little farther south.

The envoy had long since left his sickness behind and now joined the captain on the quarterdeck. Another deck chair had been constructed, and now the pair sat for hours discussing various topics. Lord Forsythe was well-travelled, with an extensive education and was able to expound upon many a subject Phillips had barely heard of. To Phillips intense relief, the subject of his wife's deliverance from her captivity never came up.

One of the subjects that did, involved the envoy's mission. Forsythe explained, "Last year a wealthy young man by the name of Bolivar, from the Spanish Province of Venezuela on the South American mainland, appeared in London and began discussing an agenda to anyone who would listen to him."

"At the Foreign Office he announced his participation in a struggle for the independence of the Spanish regions of the South American continent. He had been sent to Britain by the junta in control of the area around Caracas. His mission was to obtain recognition, arms and hopefully funding. HM government did not wish to make commitments at this stage of the game, so nothing was promised. After due consideration, Government has decided to remain strictly neutral for the time being."

"For now, the alliance with the Spanish Regency government against Napoleon is the most important item on our agenda. Later; who can tell?"

The Foreign Office had been given passports by Señor Bolivar, the Venezuelan rebel junta's representative in London. Since these were not issued by the representative of the Regency council in Spain recognized by HM government as the legitimist Spanish authority, there was doubt the regional juntas in the Spanish Americas would honor these passports. Other passports had been received from the representative in London of the Regency junta now controlling Spanish government functions on the Peninsula. It was not known if the Spanish authorities in the New World would honor these either.

Forsythe had passports from each source, but it was impossible to know in advance how they might be greeted. Using the wrong passport might well have unfortunate consequences.

Phillips deemed it necessary to reduce the usage of water. Passing through the Horse Latitudes, the trades had become uncertain, and the ship had been becalmed for hours or days at a time. The bottom tier of the big water tuns had been corrupted by the infiltration of bilge water and the water was barely drinkable.

A Marine guard was placed on the scuttle butt on deck from which the crew was accustomed to quench their thirst in the tropical heat. A small dipper had been procured from the ship's cook and crewmen were only permitted to have one dipper of water per watch.

The lack of water became more of an issue as days went by. When everyone's patience had almost expired, a cat's paw of breeze was seen ruffling the water's calm surface near the ship. The yards were hurriedly braced around, and soon Andromeda was moving. This did not last long, but soon she had another breeze, then another. Soon, the ship was sailing again. There were plenty of locations where water could be obtained, but Phillips decided to continue on toward their destination in view of the security concerns.

HMS Andromeda now was making the best of her way toward Caracas. Phillips had been advised by the Admiralty the Spanish were very sensitive about foreign ships, especially warships, in their waters. When their noon sights proclaimed they were indeed south of eighteen degrees of north latitude, Phillips called Forsythe, as well as the first officer to him on the quarterdeck and produced his sealed orders.

He asked both to examine the mildew spotted document and assure themselves the seal was still intact, after which he opened the orders and read through them rapidly. When finished, he passed them to first Lieutenant Gould and then to Forsythe. The gist of the orders were simply to determine as soon as possible after entering Spanish colonial waters, whether the area around Caracas was still in the hands of the rebels. If so, and the rebel junta was still agreeable, Lord Forsythe would disembark, while Andromeda would take on water and necessary stores.

It was ordered that no military assistance of any type should be offered to the rebels. Phillips was permitted to embark certain rebel officials if so doing would not endanger the ship or crew.

Should Spanish government forces control the area however, Captain Phillips was to attempt to determine whether another destination was appropriate. In the absence of such a port, Andromeda should sail for the nearest British port. In the interests of secrecy, it was ordered the ship not make port, whether British, Spanish or Rebel, until it was determined whether or not the outcome would be favorable. It was desirable the Spanish governmental forces in the area not discover their presence.

Both land and the sails of a large ship were sighted one morning as the sun came over the horizon. As usual when at sea, HMS Andromeda had gone to action stations just for this eventuality. The ship was hull down in the distance, but was on a course that would intersect their own. Some mountain tops were visible in the distance, which Harding said did not appear on his old chart.

Mister Gould wondered whether they should attempt to avoid the stranger, in view of the secrecy instruction of their orders. Phillips decided the newcomer had probably sighted their own ship and he did not wish to appear furtive. As the pair closed during the morning, the ensign was hoisted as was the commission pennant.

When the approaching ship hoisted Spanish Royal Colors, Phillips signaled that he was in need of water. In European waters, the Spanish Junta had been furnished copies of the basic signal code used by the Royal Navy. He had no idea of whether this code had been made known on this side of the Atlantic. When the newcomer hoisted a meaningless assemblage of flag signals, he guessed not.

By now the approaching ship had been identified by Mister Harding as la Perla de España, of forty guns, or at least one of that class. As she approached within about two cables lengths, Perla hove to, and ran out her guns.

Phillips ordered the same action, although with the disparity of force between the two ships, he knew an action would be suicidal on his part. However, he felt he must not quaver before this powerful opponent.

Through his glass, he thought he could see tendrils of smoke rising from burning match in the linstocks of the enemy. At length, an ornate launch was lowered from the Spanish frigate and a uniformed crew pulled it over to Andromeda.

The officer in her stern sheets appeared to be a teniente of the Spanish service, and Phillips ordered him piped aboard with the proper respect, Marine guard and bosun's mates present. As the officer came through the entry port he looked quickly around at the guns run out with burning match smoldering in the tubs.

Phillips answered the officer's salute and approached with Midshipman Benson by his side. Benson, he had learned, could get along in the Spanish language and would serve as translator if needed.

After each party greeted the other in his own language, it became apparent the translator would indeed be needed. After a lengthy harangue by the Spaniard, Benson reported he thought the officer was giving them notice they must leave Spanish waters immediately.

Lord Forsythe was standing in the rear and Phillips asked him to produce the passport from the Spanish junta's representative back in London. In an aside, he asked for him to be sure he had the proper one.

With some delay, Forsythe extricated the passport from his case and extended it to the officer. This person glanced at it quickly, tore it in half and threw the pieces to the wind. Another harangue followed.

The astonished mid explained the officer did not recognize this paper, it had no force here and Andromeda must immediately sail from Spanish waters.

Phillips asked the lad to explain the ship was low on water and offered to lead the officer below to examine their water stores. The teniente refused the explanation with vigorous shakes of his head.

Benson reported the officer was now going to leave, that the Perla would open fire as soon as he boarded unless this ship of heretics was standing out to sea by this time. Sending Benson below to inform the gunner, in his lair in the magazine, the ship might soon require plenty of powder cartridges, he had his officers take their places at the guns. Unhurriedly, Andromeda was stripped down to fighting sail and the ship brought to the wind on a course of ENE. This did not suit the Spaniards, since with a spout of smoke, a gun sounded angrily and a shot put up a splash just forward and short of the hull.

Not to be outdone, Phillips stood next to the forward twelve pounder and asked the gun captain, "Do you think you could pitch a shot a bit closer to her than she did to us, Higgins?"

"Aye Captain, close it is!" he muttered, sighting down the barrel. As the ship lifted on the swell, he pulled the firing lanyard just before the peak of the motion. The shot bellowed out, deafening those who had not covered their ears. The ship was now moving ahead, and for a moment Phillips thought the Spaniards might ignore them now, having made their point.

As he spotted the shot splashing just fathoms before the frigate's cutwater, her whole side erupted in smoke and flame. In return, Phillips nodded to Lieutenant Gould who ordered the guns to open on the enemy.

Surprisingly, only one shot of the barrage hit Andromeda, this one smashing through the railing amidships and showering some people with splinters. A few of Andromeda's answer splashed before the Spanish hull, but more struck. He could make out some ragged holes in the side, and the frigate's fore staysail had come adrift.

Andromeda's gun crews were in their well-rehearsed gun drill, loading the big guns like automatons. Her next broadside sounded a full minute before the Spanish answer. A ball from the Spaniard smashed through the hull and struck the base of the mizzen below deck. A carpenter's mate rushed up from below with a report. The mast was not severely injured, having only a splintered notch from a twelve pound ball in the mast's base.

The exchange kept up at a furious pace, the enemy taking half as long again to fire off a broadside as the Andromeda's. Their accuracy was improving however, and shots were coming aboard. Much of the damage was being done to their hull, not hindering the ship's sailing qualities. In contrast, a few significant hits had damaged the Perla's rigging. Her fore top mast was damaged and Phillips watched her topmen taking in canvas.

At that moment, a shot clipped the frigate's main yard. The main course pulled the damaged yard free before that canvas could be secured and now the frigate's captain had another matter to deal with.

Mister Gould wanted to turn back and try to bow rake the frigate before she could get herself back into order again.

Phillips gave the idea not a thought. His own ship had its share of damage now, and he could imagine the furor that would erupt back home if Andromeda was seriously damaged or lost. The enemy, while temporarily incapacitated, was still much larger and better armed, with a larger crew. She was by no means beaten. Had he a consort to assist, he would have continued the action. As it was, he considered it prudent to sail away and leave her alone. Long after sinking her sails below the horizon, some fishing boats were sighted off to port.

Mister Benson was called back to the quarterdeck again to try his communication skills. These fishermen spoke a patois that the lad had difficulty understanding, but one of the boats approached with a crewman that spoke a more universal type of Spanish. From this man, it was learned the revolution had probably failed. The spokesman thought Spanish forces were about to seize Caracas, although Puerto Cabello, to the west, might still be in rebel hands. Señor Bolivar had been in command there and perhaps still might be in control.

Mister Harding, the sailing master, was asked to produce his charts of the area. With little intelligence that could be relied upon, Phillips was dubious about continuing the mission, but Forsythe was in favor of continuing on to Puerto Cabello. Water was still a continuing concern. There were nearby islands, some of them originally Dutch, which had been taken by British forces. Water and other supplies could be taken on but there was the question of security.

With the disparate elements of the population, it could be almost assumed there would be people reporting to both French national sources as well as Spanish. Until Forsythe had made contact with the rebel group, it was not desirable to have knowledge of their mission leak out.

CHAPTER SEVEN

Mister Gould was of the opinion the encounter with the Spanish frigate had destroyed any chance of succeeding in their mission and they should immediately proceed to Antigua to report and re-supply.

Listening to the others, Phillips decided to follow the envoy's advice. They were not much more than a hundred miles away and would look very foolish returning to a British port, only to learn they had missed an important opportunity.

Sailing on up the coast, they saw the smoke miles before coming in sight of the port. Numerous small craft of all types were escaping the harbor, many so loaded with refugees there was little freeboard. One small fore-and-aft rigged craft they approached and asked for the news.

This was a well-appointed boat, probably a sort of yacht to some wealthy person. A prosperous looking individual on her foredeck announced in excellent English the town had fallen to government forces and he himself, Señor Simon Bolivar, was now on his way to Cartagena in New Grenada.

Apparently, the plan was to re-constitute his forces there and then continue the struggle for the independence of Venezuela.

Phillips enquired if Señor Bolivar would wish to travel to New Grenada in HMS Andromeda, but the rebel leader assured him he was comfortable in his present craft, but he would welcome an escort if that were possible. HMS Andromeda escorted the vessel to Cartagena, where Lord Forsythe decided to leave the ship and put himself in the hands of Bolivar. Phillips had some misgivings about leaving the rather helpless individual alone in a torn country, but the fellow was an envoy and had his job to do.

Promising Forsythe he would mention his situation to the British authorities at any station he touched at, they made their farewells and Andromeda put out to sea.

The mission now complete, Mister Harding set sail. The first order of business was to secure water. The men had been on short rations for too long and their welfare must be considered. Of course, in the absence of Spanish shore installations or ships of war, it ought to be possible to land the ship's boats in either Cartagena itself or in some shore-side creek mouth on the mainland and load water there.

However, fever was prevalent in these regions, and Aruba, a former Dutch island close by was another possibility. It had a drier climate and British forces had taken the island soon after the war resumed when the Treaty of Amiens had ran its course. Phillips knew there was now a British presence on the island, and he should at least be able to obtain water.

With no encounters with anything larger than small fishing vessels, the ship made her way to Fort Zoutman on the western side of the island. There, Phillips reported to the British garrison commander. He learned there had been no serious obstacles to the British occupation of the island since its seizure from the Dutch after the renewal of the war. There were some dis-affected citizenry in the area but they had presented no major problems so far. Water was available, and the crew members were given their fill the first day from the quantities of fresh water brought aboard.

With limited shore leave granted for the hands, there was a chance for the men to remove themselves from ship's discipline for a few hours. Mister Gould wondered about the wisdom of giving the men the opportunity to desert, but Phillips reasoned any men who drifted away could be easily gathered up again with the assistance of the Army garrison.

Actually, the ship gained a few men. A small, dilapidated fishing boat came alongside the anchored Andromeda just before dawn, a day after anchoring, its Black crew wishing to join. These were all slaves of a local owner. Only one of the newcomers could speak English. This individual was a servant of the fishing boat's owner who had been purchased on one of the British Windward Islands, and could speak the English dialect prevalent there.

An investigation found these men fished for their Dutch owner who had the catch salted down to feed his other slaves. They were required to be out daily in their flimsy boat in all kinds of weather with the hurricane season now upon them. These men had, of course, no formal education, but all were careful seafarers. They knew the sea and the winds and some were able to make educated guesses of tomorrow's weather. Nevertheless, the owner insisted they go out to sea in fair weather or foul.

After some debate amongst themselves, it was concluded if they must go to sea, it would be better to do so in a well-built ship. There was a certain amount of hesitation, but some felt their lives were forfeit anyway, so they might just as well test their fate on a King's ship.

Phillips had to consider the situation. Of course, the protests of the Dutch owner need not necessarily be given much weight, but the British commander of the garrison might not wish to incur antagonism with his subjects and decide to order him to return the slaves to their owner. A discussion with Mister Harding followed. The forthcoming weather was debated and it was the sailing master that predicted a blow would manifest itself soon.

Accordingly, Mister Gould read the new men in and they were assigned to watches. No one expected the new hands to be especially useful for a period. All were exceedingly thin, almost emaciated. All were horribly scarred with lash wounds. Doctor Baynes, who had remained on the ship after losing his prime patient, pronounced himself outraged at the condition of the men, and refused to allow them to do any physical work for at least a week. They were committed to Doctor Baynes' care and were not permitted to appear on deck while in harbor.

The barest mention of the voluntary recruitment of the men was entered into the log, with no mention made as to their previous condition of servitude and no mention was made to the garrison commander or the slaves' owner. Each of the new hands was given a new English-sounding name which was entered in the log. Hopefully, there would not be more than a cursory inspection of the log months later at the end of the voyage.

Andromeda's launch was hoisted over the side and set out under sail on the early land breeze, towing the empty fishing boat to sea. Out of sight of land, the craft would be cast loose and left to the whims of the current.

There were very limited resources for ship repair on the island. But a few island cattle, small and thin, were purchased for consumption by the crew. Salt was available, and the hands, except for the former slaves, were set to work butchering and salting down the meat. Then it was time to depart. The only mention made of the missing slaves or their boat was a comment by the military commander to be on the lookout for a missing fishing boat and crew, feared lost in the recent blow.

Making their way up the chain of islands, they came to Antigua where Captain Phillips saluted the flag of Governor Eliot and learned the admiral of that station was at sea.

Reporting to Government House, he had his audience with Eliot and handed over all the documents concerning his last mission. Eliot, who had known Lord Forsythe previously, was concerned about the envoy's safety, and assured Phillips he would endeavor to determine the safety of Forsythe, whenever possible.

In the meantime, he informed Phillips, the United States had declared war against Britain, and he should govern his actions accordingly. For now, Governor Eliot thought HMS Andromeda should be sent to Halifax where her further use could better be assessed.

CHAPTER EIGHT

Several American merchantmen were encountered on the voyage north. He had no instructions as to his actions against the new adversary. He was well aware of the pre-war tensions between the two nations and realized the indiscriminate pressing of seamen from American shipping was a prime cause of the discontent. Of course, the harboring of deserters from the Royal Navy aboard the same shipping was another. Deciding not to do anything that might tend to inflame the situation, he remained clear of the merchantmen and continued on.

Off New York, a large schooner approached, flying the American flag, with her guns run out. She was to windward, to the west of Andromeda, and was free to do as she wished. She was situated so that she could run with the wind, almost surely outpacing Andromeda.

Phillips ordered his own guns run out. His ensign was flying as was his commission pennant, so the stranger could have been in no doubt as to his status.

The schooner immediately put herself about, sailing several points into the wind closer than Andromeda could be expected to manage. She nimbly dodged Andromeda and sailed back toward New York. Phillips ignored the stranger. He guessed this to be a privateer, rigged out hastily on the declaration of war. Until he could get some guidance for his actions however, he decided to let her go.

It was doubtful he could come up to her anyway, and he had no wish to become tangled in the near shore coastline of the United States, of which he had insufficient charts.

It was with some relief they saluted the flag of Admiral Sawyer on entry to Halifax. Phillips was pulled ashore to the admiral's shore side office where he spent an hour being briefed upon the situation.

He learned that not all Americans were vehemently in favor of the war. Many people, especially those in the shipping trade, were opposed to it. Much of the food exports from the United States, especially grain and beef, were being shipped up the New England coast to Canada or across the Atlantic. Wellington's forces, now fully engaged with the French on the Iberian Peninsula, were largely being fed by these imports from America.

It was desirable to refrain from angering these potential allies by ill-considered actions. On the other hand, American privateers were fitting out by the hundreds, and the West India convoy was expected to be approaching Bermuda soon. This convoy must be protected at all cost. A serious loss from that convoy, could bring financial disaster to London. Therefore, Andromeda was to be hurriedly supplied with needed provisions, water and other needed gear and sent on her way to locate the convoy and provide such protection as possible.

Any privateers met should be prosecuted, but he must not go haring off on long chases if that might interfere with locating the convoy. Any merchantmen encountered should be examined closely to determine their destination. If bound for a French port, they were certainly to be seized. However, any sailing to a port controlled by Wellington or the Spanish Regency in Spain or in Portugal or any British port were to be sent on their way without hindrance.

The mizzen damaged in the encounter with the Spanish frigate was to be replaced. Spars were available in plenty here, and although it was not considered an emergency repair, it was decided to do the task now rather than wait until it did become an emergency. The dockyard superintendent indicated replacing the mast, along with setting up the standing and running rigging along with other necessary repairs would take a week, all men working to capacity.

While the work was in progress, Phillips decided to wander about the shops here to see what was available and stock up on cabin stores. He had negotiated a bill of exchange while in southern waters and now possessed a satisfactory store of Spanish dollars, such coin being in demand in a specie starved port such as Halifax.

He took with him one of the former slaves taken aboard in Aruba. This man Nero, had been savagely whipped at one time, which had so injured his body he was no longer capable of heavy work about ship. Phillips was using him as his servant, a task which he performed well. Hiring a two wheeled cart and driver, the two went off to do their shopping. It was a fine day and all seemed well. A chandler's shop offered all the cabin stores Phillips needed, and Nero directed the staff in stowing the articles in the cart. Among the supplies purchased was a store of Spanish cigars, of which Phillips secured several before sending everything else back to the ship, escorted by Nero.

Phillips found a light for his cigar, and began strolling about the town. Passing a weather beaten building with a sign above the door proclaiming it sold fine guns, he went inside. The proprietor was a young Scottish gun maker, recently come to the new world. His inventory was small, but Phillips was drawn to a pair of pistols on the counter. Their rather plain, outward appearance was unlike any other firearm he had ever seen. The ordinary assemblage of pan, cock and frizzen was missing. Instead, a small, discrete hammer-like affair was present and little else.

Mister Campbell explained. He told Phillips how a Scottish clergyman had invented a new ignition system for firearms using fulminate of mercury. This substance, when struck sharply, exploded and was capable of firing the powder charge in a firearm. The inventor had been having difficulty in utilizing the highly explosive substance though.

As a journeyman gun maker, Mister Campbell was employed by the clergyman to do much of the skilled work. One of his tasks was to find a better way to utilize the new ignition system in a safer manner.

Early on, Campbell had made a simple swage into which he could place little sheet copper disks and with a sharp rap from a hammer, form tiny cups into which he could place small amounts of fulminate. Sealed in with a drop of varnish, the little cups were nearly waterproof.

Expanding on his invention, he then developed a steel nipple upon which the cap could be placed. The nipple would be screwed into a forging at the breech of the gun. A passageway communicated through the forging to the weapon's powder charge. The weapon's hammer, which replaced the cock on a normal flintlock gun, upon striking the cap, exploded it, the flash then entering the weapon's chamber via the passageway and firing the main charge.

The ignition was faster and more certain than the old flintlock system. The clergyman had not been available much of the time Campbell had been working on the device, and had no great expectations for it.

He was available however, when a stern-faced father approached the workshop with a sobbing daughter in trail and demanded to know what Mister Campbell had to say to explain why his daughter's clothing was now much too tight.

The clergyman, of course, could not have one of his employees engaging in such licentious behavior, and dismissed him on the spot.

Not to be denied, the insistent parent followed Campbell from the shop where Campbell assured him he would marry the young woman, however without a livelihood now, he had no idea of how to support her. The now mollified father, relieved at the prospect of securing a husband for his daughter, questioned Campbell at some length about his qualifications in the gun-making trade. Assured, he offered to pay the passage of the couple to Canada, where his skills would likely be in demand.

Campbell was indeed successful, and soon had a shop of his own, along with a new daughter, after his bride came to term. He repaired weapons for hunters and military officers and made a few new ones based on the new ignition system. These were not as successful as he had hoped. He himself was the only source of the necessary percussion caps, and hunters or officers might find it difficult to replace the item when needed. Flints for the old system were available anywhere.

The new system intrigued Phillips when it was explained to him. It could be an embarrassing situation when a firearm refused to fire in the heat of an engagement, and this seemed to make that event more unlikely.

To that end, he purchased the pair of pistols on display and ordered a thousand of the special caps made up. Campbell assured him he would put his newly appointed apprentice to work on the task immediately, and have the stock ready before Andromeda sailed.

Elated to have sold the pistols he had formerly feared would remain on his inventory for months, he made an additional attempt at another sale. Months before, a British officer had brought a weapon into his shop for repair. The officer had been serving with Sir Isaac Brock, and had been based in Upper Canada. Serving with Native American tribes in disputed territory to the south, he had brought back a strange rifle. He had traded a dozen blankets and two pounds of gunpowder to a Shawnee warrior for it. It had been taken from an American settler in one of the incessant raids of those days.

Originally made in Lancaster, Pennsylvania, by a local gun maker there, it was a rather handsome piece. With an exceedingly long barrel and figured maple stock, it seemed a strange weapon for the rigors of combat in the wilderness. The lock of this weapon was broken, and the bullet mold missing. In this condition, the rifle was of no immediate use to the officer.

The officer wondered if repair was feasible. Campbell had assured him it could be done, but not in the time frame the officer required. The officer, who was destined to leave in a week in a convoy back to England, traded the weapon for a pair of pocket pistols and left the rifle to Campbell to do with as he wished.

Still believing he could make a success of his new ignition system, the gun maker made a new lock of that persuasion and fitted it to the rifle. The gun barrel, with its worn rifling, was bored out to a slightly larger caliber and re-rifled. With fresh balls cast from a new bullet mold, the rifle was in all important respects a new piece. With no buyers apparent, he made a pitch to sell the weapon to this new customer. Leading Phillips out the rear door, he pointed to a block of crumbling rock nearly two hundred yards distant.

Campbell explained the loading of the rifle. From a leather hunting bag he produced a paper cartridge containing a measured charge of powder, a greased patch and a single lead ball. He opened the little packet and poured the powder down the muzzle. Discarding the paper remnants, he placed the patch over the muzzle and centered the ball on that. Pushing the ball and patch into the bore with a short rod, he removed the longer ramrod from under the barrel. Pressure applied to this pushed the charge all the way to the breach.

With his finger, he opened a little brass door on the side of the buttstock and extracted a single cap of his own manufacture and placed it on the ignition nipple.

He explained to Phillips the rifle was now ready to fire. He indicated he was intending to fire at the distant rock and asked his potential customer to watch for the impact of the ball on the rock.

Phillips was not un-familiar with rifles, his father owning one that he had fired frequently in his youth. However, he observed as Campbell took careful aim and squeezed off his shot. With his father's weapon, there would have been a noticeable delay between the flash of the powder in the pan and the discharge of the weapon. There was no such delay with this rifle. At the fall of the hammer, the rifle cracked almost instantly and a puff of rock dust flew from the stone down range.

Phillips loaded and fired a few rounds himself and pronounced himself satisfied. Back in the shop, he counted out the Spanish dollars required for the purchase of the pistols and the rifle and placed an extra order for the necessary caps and balls to fit the new weapons.

Campbell promised to have everything aboard Andromeda before the week was out. Leaving the rifle behind for cleaning, Phillips took his pistols with him and returned to the ship.

CHAPTER NINE

Andromeda had been kedged back to her mooring and was nearly ready to sail when a shabby little skiff was pulled up to her port beam and the gun maker's apprentice passed up the rifle and package of ammunition to the anchor watch. Returning from another visit ashore, Phillips examined the weapon and was satisfied with his purchase. Enlisting the service of the new Royal Marine officer, Lieutenant Daniels, who had come aboard in Halifax, he went onto the quarterdeck to see what opportunities presented themselves to test the rifle.

Gulls were wheeling about overhead, and several were perched on pilings protruding from the water. The birds were at respectable distances and neither officer expected to hit one of them.

Daniels was most enthused about the new ignition system. At sea, firing a flint lock weapon was often dubious because of spray. If the powder in a pan became damp, the weapon would surely not fire until the priming, at least, was replaced. These caps seemed to fire every time though.

The gulls did not seem unduly perturbed by the target practice. After the first few shots, most of the birds ignored the discharges unless a ball passed too close. Finally, Daniels managed to strike a bird at nearly one hundred yards distance. The ruined bird fell thrashing into the sea and the remainder departed for a safer environment.

Mister Daniels volunteered his servant, a Royal Marine private, to clean the rifle, and Phillips called over his first officer to discuss the ship's next voyage. The visit ashore with Vice Admiral Sawyer had produced his sailing orders and his instructions. American privateers were swarming to sea all along the eastern seaboard, with the intent to savage British trade. He was to attempt to disrupt this activity as much as was possible.

American shipping had in the recent past been of great importance to Britain and its action in Spain and Portugal. The harvest in Britain had been poor in recent seasons and prices were climbing daily for needed farm produce. Any American shipping, wishing to continue that trade, should be encouraged. For now, no pressing of seamen from these ships would be countenanced.

However, those American ships attempting trade with France or with French forces wherever found should be taken as prizes, the ships brought to a British port if possible, else they should be destroyed.

Any American ships encountered at sea, should be closely examined to determine their destination.

One of the final projects he had done in the dockyard was painting ship. A previous cargo from home landed from the last convoy was paint. With his own funds, Phillips purchased enough brown paint to give the ship's sides a coat. From his place on the quarterdeck, he overheard a pair of midshipmen passing in a launch comparing the post ship to an old barn. Mister Darby, the second officer, was present and outraged at the effrontery of the young men. He clearly wished Captain Phillips to summon them aboard to have their ears roasted, but Phillips smiled and ignored the event. Truthfully, he hoped any Yankee privateers they encountered would think the same. Surely, no King's ship, would put to sea in such a state.

The new paint covered the gun port lids, and from a distance the closed ports were not apparent. From the chandler's, he had procured some old barrels and crates which could be strategically placed around the deck, making the post ship appear to be a small down-at-the-heels trader.

To gild the lily, some cast off sailcloth was obtained from the dockyard. This was old, thin stuff with multiple patches. Already condemned and destined to be destroyed because of its condition, the dockyard master was willing to sell it for a small sum. The sailmaker set to with his crew cutting the poor material to fit.

At the last minute before sailing, a draft of seventy men was put on board launches and pulled out to Andromeda. These were mostly involuntary levies from the other ships in harbor, although some were volunteer landsmen, succumbing to the tales of wealth likely to be garnered from all of the American prizes taken.

HMS Andromeda was pulled out of harbor by her headsails. Initially, Phillips intended to follow the trade route merchant shipping generally followed on the way to the Channel. He had hoped to join up with a convoy, but the next was not due for weeks yet, and Vice-Admiral Sawyer was explicit with the necessity for her to depart as soon as possible. The first matter on the agenda was to look for enemy privateers. After several weeks of that, it would be time to search for the next convoy from home. He hoped to meet up with that shipping near Bermuda, but he well knew there was always the possibility they would miss each other. He would have been more comfortable with several more ships. However, he must make do with what he had.

One problem with travelling alone was, according to a recent Order in Council, British commercial shipping was forbidden to sail unless in convoy. This action had been taken soon after the American declaration of war had been received in London. Thus, posing as a lone British merchantman might be suspicious.

Mister Harding voiced his doubts about the effectiveness of the disguise, but Goodrich, the third officer assured him a previous Order in Council had removed the requirement of sailing in convoy because of the elimination of the French threat in the Caribbean. It was only after the American entry into the war that it was re-imposed. "Who is to say we did not sail before we learned of the new order", Goodrich assured the sailing master.

After making their offing, the ship was readied for the closest inspection by a marauding privateer. The tops'ls were replaced by the ancient canvas secured from the dockyard. It had been reinforced by the sailmaker so no splits were likely to occur at in-opportune moments. The ship's cook got into the act by throwing some visibly noxious substance over the side, leaving an unsightly stripe down to the waterline.

Some of the empty boxes and casks secured ashore were place strategically about on the weather deck. The remainder were disassembled and struck below into the hold. In the event the ship would clear for action, the material on deck could be thrown over the side in a minute.

The hands entered into the scheme with a will, often coming up with their own notions. Despite this however, Andromeda was not a universally happy ship. The extra draft of men taken aboard severely strained the living space in the berth deck. Then too, some of the levied men were those their old captains thought they could well do without. Already, the sea lawyers among them were muttering about their outrageous transfer away from the old ship and mates. The landsmen had not had the opportunity to be disgruntled yet. Most of them were too incapacitated from sea-sickness.

Phillips had asked Admiral Sawyer for the extra men. He had thought if he took several prizes, the extra hands would come in handy to man them. Otherwise, captured ships would necessarily be torched. Now though, with the new turmoil on his previously well-ordered ship, he was not so sure he had done the right thing. On the third day out, he had about come to the conclusion he must start flogging some men, if but to just get their attention. There had been some downright disobedience toward his officers and petty officers, and names had been taken.

He mentioned to Mister Gould, who was standing on the quarterdeck, just aft of a party of men holystoning the deck early one morning, that it was time to have a mast for defaulters. He knew this would be discussed by the men on the berth deck on their off watch.

Late in the fore-noon watch that day, the masthead lookout reported a sail approaching on their starboard beam. He soon advised the stranger to be ship rigged but was still hull down. It seemed to be altering course to intercept their own.

Phillips did not regard this as unusual. The likely explanation was a King's ship coming up from southerly regions. As he went to his quarters, after taking the noon sights, everyone on the ship with a glass was leaning over the rail to examine the sail plan of the newcomer to see if she could be identified.

It was his second officer, Mister Darby who reported hesitantly, and announced. "Sir, we do not think this sighting to be a King's ship. Her rig is not what we would expect to see on such. I myself have never seen her before, I am sure. Some of us are thinking she may be a Yankee privateer."

"Well Mister Darby, you cannot say we look all that much like one of His Majesty's ships, ourselves. However, you could very well be correct. I will be on deck shortly."

On deck, the stranger had distinctly closed. She was now over the horizon and the details of her hull were becoming apparent. She appeared to be a rather large, ship rigged vessel, probably not new, but spacious enough to carry either a large cargo or plenty of men. From her inquisitive nature, Phillips would have wagered on her carrying more men than cargo.

It was unlikely for a timid merchantman to approach a strange sighting so boldly. It could be she was a merchantman with a letter of marque. These documents, Phillips had been informed, were being issued by the hundreds from every port on the American seaboard. Such a document would allow a trading ship carrying cargo, to take prizes, provided the ship had a few guns and enough men to take the risk.

At any rate, Andromeda could not continue sailing along fat and dumb, waiting for the stranger to close. There was every chance she would smell a rat and sheer away. Sailing in light westerly breezes under her ancient topsails, Phillips gave orders to set the fore and main courses. These were no better than the tops'ls, being old, discarded sailcloth gleaned from the dockyard scrap, of the type a parsimonious owner might choose to equip an old ship.

With the extra canvas, the ship began showing a wake, but with some judicious work at the braces, enough wind was spilled to allow the stranger to slowly continue to come up. It was coming on close to sunset when the pursuer hoisted her flag and fired a gun. It was a Yankee, and the gun she fired appeared to be a nine pounder long gun.

CHAPTER TEN

Phillips ordered all plain sail set, and the yards braced to the wind. Before the sun set, it was now certain Andromeda was holding her own, neither gaining nor falling behind. The sky was overcast and no moon was present, so for the moment, at least, they were out of sight of their pursuer. Satisfied, called his officers into the cabin along with the bosun's mate of the watch.

"Gentlemen, I wish to set before you what I hope will happen. Of course we are all aware a Yankee privateer is close behind us with a powerful ship, likely full of men. We could come about now and engage her with a most likely positive result. We might well lose more men than I would wish by engaging in the dark though, so I propose to wait until dawn, when we shall make the attempt in the morning light with our men rested."

"Hopefully, the enemy believes us to be a ragged merchantman, barely able to stay out of his clutches. Likely he will stay with us as best he can in hopes of getting a few shots into us. I want to assist him in keeping us in sight, but of course I will not allow him to close or fire into us."

"Thus, now that he can no longer see us, I will take down our old canvas and hoist our good sailcloth, taking care to not fall behind. As soon as that is finished, we will begin to encourage our pursuer. Presently, we are darkened so that it is difficult for her to see us. Therefore, we will begin making some mistakes."

"Mister Gladding", Phillips ordered, addressing the bosun's mate of the watch. "Occasionally, one of your men will wish to light his pipe. He may do this from the binnacle light, which is of course now shuttered, to keep it from the view of the enemy. By opening the shutter, the people behind us will get a quick glimpse of the light, enough to determine our position. This must seem accidental, so as not to invoke suspicion."

"The deck officer may also feel the need of tobacco. Therefore, I am leaving a supply of Spanish cigars by the helm. At his discretion, he, as well as the helmsmen, may wish to smoke also. As with the men forward, they may light their cigars from the binnacle lamp, making certain the shutter is closed when finished."

"Soon after we have disclosed our position to our followers, we will make a course change to port, as if we are attempting to draw away. Before we get too far away however, it will be necessary to 'accidentally' disclose our new position once again."

"While this is going on, I would like our deck cleared of all of our trash. It should be taken down and struck below. I do not wish it thrown overboard just yet for fear of alerting the enemy."

"Before first light, we will clear for action, and see what we can attempt with the enemy. Are we all clear, gentlemen?"

During the black night, Andromeda made her twists and turns, only to be followed by her pursuer. It was only in the early part of the morning watch that sufficient light discipline was able to be imposed that she could now remain completely out of sight. Phillips, assured the ship was in good hands, got a few hours of sleep. It was still black outside, when he was awakened by the morning watch coming on deck. He was on deck before the crew came to tear apart his quarters as was their duty in clearing the ship for action.

A bleary Lieutenant Daniels greeted him as he gained the quarterdeck. It seemed neither of the watch officers on duty that night were smokers. So the Marine had remained on deck all night, smoking one cigar after another. He reported his mouth and throat were foul and he was never going to smoke another cigar again.

All his officers were on deck, and it was Mister Harding who pointed out the enemy. She had ranged up during the evening, and was now approaching the starboard beam, still well astern. The ship was mostly invisible, but the sailing master pointed out an infinitely small sporadic twinkle at her helm as someone sucked on his pipe. Harding chuckled. "Sir, we aren't the only ones smoking on duty."

The enemy was right to windward, so Phillips knew the fresh breeze would blow any slight noise made aboard Andromeda right away. He told his officers and midshipmen he wanted the ship brought to stations with guns run out, as quietly as possible. Matches were not to be lit in the darkness. Instead, the flintlock firing mechanisms would be relied upon until action commenced.

At the point when he judged the lightening sky would begin to reveal him clearly to the privateer, he ordered his ship stripped to fighting sail, with the courses furled, and the fore tops'l laid aback. The ship slowed to almost a halt in the sea and waited for her pursuer to come booming up.

Come up she did, her cutwater throwing the sea at her prow aside in a white mustache, all doubts of her prey's location dispelled. One of the stranger's guns up forward slammed, and the ball struck perilously close to Andromeda's bow.

At that point, Phillips nodded to Mister Gould, and the broadside crashed, all guns firing almost simultaneously. At cable's length range, most shots struck, and ruin struck the enemy ship. Men were smashed to red jam, guns torn from carriages, and equipment smashed. The surviving members of the enemy crew were transformed instantly from a confident unit expecting to receive the surrender of a helpless foe into crippled, beaten individuals.

A few guns from the privateer's broadside fired in reply, but it was too little, too late. As guns were reloaded on Andromeda, they began their savage duty, pounding their iron balls into the privateer. With her foremast and bowsprit now down, the helpless ship began drifting toward Andromeda.

Aware of the masses of men often aboard these privateers, Phillips ordered his guns to shift from firing ball to grape, this being more effective against personnel. After a blast of that medicine, he then ordered the tops'l yards braced around and the ship put to the wind. She came around the bow of the stricken ship and again backed her tops'ls with her guns run out, offering to bow rake the privateer.

With no escape possible, the ship lowered her flag and surrendered.

CHAPTER ELEVEN

Still laying athwart the privateer's bow, Phillips sent the launch and cutter to the vessel, each full of armed seamen and Marines. Mister Goodrich, aboard the privateer which bore the name of the Captain Lawrence who had commanded the Chesapeake when she had been assaulted by HMS Shannon, shouted from her forecastle that the doctor was needed. Doctor Baynes was fully occupied with tending his own wounded, a few of whom were serious indeed. However, at the urging of his captain, he left them in the charge of his rather capable loblolly boy and was pulled over in the jolly boat.

It was a horrible shambles on board the prize. She had set out to sea with her hull packed with as many men as she could cram aboard. Her captain and owners had anticipated entering a prize-rich sea, where their ship would be the wolf attacking the flocks of dozens of helpless British merchant ships.

Her numerous crew were intended to man the many prizes she expected to make, while not weakening herself in case she did have to defend herself against some small British warship. Instead though, before making a single capture, she herself had entered combat with a capable British frigate. The numerous casualties were a result of all those people crowded together being fired into at close range by Andromeda's guns.

All of them were fodder for the terrible balls and grapeshot that came relentlessly aboard. Of the more than three hundred people on board when the action started, only a hundred were still relatively whole now. Eighty men had gone over the side, and many more were expected to as the dozens of horribly wounded expired.

The prize did have a doctor aboard, although Doctor Baynes assured his captain this fellow had only served an abbreviated apprenticeship, and would never be considered qualified back home. As the two ship's surgeons served hour after hour to alleviate what pain they could, more patients died continuously.

At first, there was nothing to give the men for their pain save quantities of rum, but eventually, in the cabin of the privateer's captain, there was found a quantity of laudanum. This substance Doctor Baynes reported, was opium that had been dissolved in refined spirits. The doctor reported it to be a specific for pain, but was not always used because of its cost and the possibility of the user becoming addicted to its use. An improper dosage could also be dangerous.

Apparently, the ship's captain before being cut nearly in half by a ball during the action, had not trusted his inexperienced surgeon with its use and locked it away.

The Sick and Hurt Board did not furnish such medicaments to its ship's surgeons. Doctor Baynes, from his civilian practice, was familiar with the substance but had not thought to bring any along on the voyage, assuming the ship would have adequate resources to treat its people.

At any rate, he took charge of the laudanum and began treating the wounded aboard both ships with the panacea.

The weather began to intensify after the action, and the motion of both ships was becoming lively. Seamen from both sides were put to the task of rigging a jury foremast and bowsprit for the prize. Her first officer, left in charge of his own men by the death of his captain, begged Phillips to send the prize into port. Hopefully Boston, but Halifax would do. Phillips had to explain to the man his concern the ship would return to her privateering career should he send her into Boston.

As far as Halifax was concerned, it would be a trying voyage, beating into the prevailing wind with her cargo of desperately wounded men. He had to consider a possible attempt to re-take the ship. In any case, he would lose the crew he put in the ship to sail her back. The American was informed the prize would accompany Andromeda on her voyage.

It was a strange looking prize that took station in Andromeda's wake. The Lawrence had carried a pair of good Maine spars aboard, just in case of this eventuality. One of them was put to use as her new foremast, with an exotic looking lateen mounted on it. The remnants of her fore topmast did duty as her new bowsprit.

Before setting out, Phillips went aboard in the now blustery weather to examine the prize. Most of the more serious damage had been attended to. A prize crew just sufficient to sail the ship was present, but Mister

Goodrich, commanding the prize, was concerned that in a blow he might be short of hands. He suggested, "Sir, I have served in the Royal Navy for ten years now. I have recognized a half dozen men among the American crew whom I recognized as British seamen that I have sailed with in the past.'

"I have not said anything to any of them, but I know they will be facing severe punishment when we make port and they are identified as deserters serving against their country. Could we perhaps ask them to serve their country again and maybe have their recent indiscretions overlooked?"

After some thought, Phillips ordered his Royal Marine sergeant to deliver the named individuals to the quarterdeck. All six looked rightfully alarmed when they were paraded aft. He explained to them their secret was out, and they should know the penalty for desertion and for fighting against their own country. None had anything to say.

To their silence, Phillips offered. "Davison there, I remember you sailed on the Resolve when my father had her. I was a mid at the time. I have not the slightest desire to see you flogged to death or run up to the yardarm. But what in hell am I to do with you men? If I let you off, others will think they too have a right to walk away from the ship whenever they wish."

With no reply coming from the men, Phillips told them. "As it happens, I do have an idea. It is foolish, I know, and will probably cost me my commission. However, we will give it a try."

"I need hands on my ship. Skilled able seamen who can hand, reef and steer. I am going to ask for volunteers from the crew of the Lawrence, as many of us do when taking prizes. You men can volunteer. You will not use your own names to sign on however. You will be a completely different seaman than the one who deserted from his old ship. You will keep your mouths shut about this, and perhaps we all may just survive. Any questions?"

"Sir, your honor", Davison began. "There are men aboard Andromeda who know us. Mister Goodrich here was a snotty on one of my old ships. The truth will come out."

"Davison, half the men on my ship have names their parents did not give them. Your mates will keep their mouths shut, unless they wish to see you hang. My officers will also, on my order. If you sign on and work with a will you may yet to live to see grandchildren. Now, when you sign on as volunteers, I will put you aboard Andromeda. I do not want your old mates on the Lawrence to tempt you away from your duty. I will bring other hands back here in your place. Now, are we clear on this?"

As the ships continued the search for privateers, the crews began to settle down. When Phillips was sure there would be no trouble with the prize, he had her sail off to port with a good ten miles separation between the ships to extend their search area.

The British deserters aboard the prize had all volunteered under new names and had been duly logged in. Even a few Americans signed on, to avoid a stint in a prison hulk. Most of the Americans though, were outraged at the perfidy of their former shipmates who had turned on them. Previously, many of these seamen had been employed in doing essential ship's work on both vessels and had been given relatively loose rein, but now the growing tensions between the differing groups required the healthy Americans to be battened below decks on the two ships.

It was with much relief when the convoy they were searching for slid over the horizon just north of Bermuda.

There was some suspicion at first from the escorting ships of that convoy. Andromeda's brown sides and the threadbare sails did not induce confidence in the escorts, especially the Titan 64, commanded by Captain Raton, a very senior officer near the top of the post captain's list.

Phillips found himself standing in front of Raton's desk explaining Andromeda's appearance. The frankly dubious Raton finally dismissed him but required he search for a convoy member which had come missing after an attack by a pair of Yankee privateers.

Raton was unwilling to give more information, but once back on deck, an old friend from Resolve, now fourth lieutenant aboard Titan, gave him the hurried story.

In the teeth of a blow two days back, a pair of big Yankee schooners had come out of a rain squall and pounced on the convoy. Titan remained at her station to windward of the leading column. There were two other escorts, a non-rated brig in the rear and an armed cutter midway up the lee column. One schooner made a feint against the shipping to the rear and was fended off by the brig. Another came to the center and burst into the column, scattering it. The cutter attempted to send that predator off but was dismasted in the exchange and left behind. Both schooners then pursued a single brig, carrying general cargo and a few passengers that had separated from the main flock. Caught up in a new rain squall, neither the merchantman nor the privateers had been seen again.

Phillips was pulled back to Andromeda and told his officers of his chastening from the liner's captain. One positive development he was able to inform them. He was to leave his prize and the captive crew in the charge of Captain Raton. Head money would be due to the Andromeda's crew for the captive crew taken from the Lawrence, Five pounds a head. Phillips suspected Raton would try to fiddle matters so Titan would get the head money and perhaps make a try at the prize money also. At any rate, that was a matter for the future. Now he had a missing brig to search for, plus a pair of privateers.

With the captured American ship safely in the middle of a convoy, Phillips felt he could remove some of his prize crew, being confident the American's would not make a bid for escape, while surrounded, as they were.

Reasoning that the brig, if still free, would likely make for the nearest port, in this case Halifax, Phillips set a course for that port. He felt he had followed his orders thus far. He had taken a Yankee privateer, found the convoy, and had been sent away from that on what he regarded as a fool's mission.

He decided he would run down the latitude line to Halifax to see if he could find the missing brig. Should that not work, he would work against the Gulf Stream to the south, checking into the possibility that the brig had been taken by the schooners and sent into Boston.

Finding nothing, he went south. Finally, down in American waters, he ran her down. The Sarah Hayes, a British brig had been taken shortly after she had left the convoy. The brig was now alone, with just her American prize crew and some of the original crew aboard. Sending his own crew aboard, he had everyone else brought on Andromeda. Interviewing the American crew, nothing important was learned. The American prize crew refused to divulge any information of the parent schooners or where they might be patrolling.

Phillips ordered them below, and had the brig's original crew brought in. Two were missing, and reported by their former captain to have joined the Americans. Asked for their ideas, all were forthright.

As Captain Lawton explained, "They had us for a while in a little hole built right up in the foc's'le of the schooner that took us. We could hear them talking well enough. It sounded like they were waiting for the other schooner to come back from a chase she was on, and then they were going to send us into port in the brig and the pair of them would then go off to try their luck in the Channel, back home."

"They were going to take Miss Humphrey off the brig, put us back on and they were going to be off."

"Just a minute, Captain Lawton. Just who is this Miss Humphrey, you mentioned?"

"Her? She is the owner's daughter. Mister Humphrey took her to sea, when her mother died. Then, during the chase, a ball from the four pounder that one of the schooners fired, took off his arm. Our first mate bound it up, but Mister Humphries lost too much blood and he died."

"I heard one of the privateers men say they were going to send the brig in to port, and see if they could ransom Miss Humphries."

CHAPTER TWELVE

Captain Larson was sent aboard the Sarah Hayes and a prize crew commanded by a midshipman was put aboard, ordered to take the brig to Halifax. The remainder of the original crew was pressed into the Navy and would serve aboard Andromeda. The post ship was put on the course that would follow normal shipping lanes to the Channel entrance across the Atlantic.

As Phillips explained to his sailing master, he intended to follow the pair of privateers, if possible taking them, if not, they could at least spread the word of their presence.

The sailing master wondered what they could do about the woman taken from the brig. Phillips answered, "I don't see how we can do much, Mister Harding, unless we manage to take the schooner she is aboard. Apparently, they mean to ransom her. To do that, they will need to get a message ashore somehow with their demands and the payment method. This all could take months, and I expect they will either be back in America by then or possibly taken."

The ship continued on course for days without sighting another ship. Then, almost two weeks after leaving the Sarah Hayes, two sails were spotted ahead. Both were moderate sized ship-rigged merchant vessels flying the American flag. Heavily laden, they were run down with no difficulty and brought to heel.

Mister Otis, acting as third lieutenant, in the absence of Mister Goodrich, went aboard the Boston Commerce and reported she was laden with wheat, destined for Portugal. The second ship, Rebecca Morris, was also laden with the same cargo, but additionally carried a deck-cargo of spars. Deciding to inspect this one himself, Phillips left Mister Gould in charge and was pulled over in his gig.

The captain of the merchantman was decidedly nervous. He knew well he could find his ship taken prize and himself on his way to a hulk very soon. Keeping his silence, Captain Phillips had Mister Otis lead him to the cabin where the manifest and ship's log were laid out on a small table.

The ship ostensibly was destined to make port in South Carolina where she would offer her cargo in trade. Instead, here she was in mid-Atlantic heading for Europe. Questioned, the captain told him this cargo was his own private venture. Rumors abounded in Boston there was an excellent market for American wheat in Lisbon, and good straight spars were also bringing respectable prices. The American government had placed an embargo on the export of certain goods important for Britain's economy.

The American captain was concerned the American government would not take kindly to his commercial activities, since they could be construed as aiding the enemy. So, his manifest indicated he was taking the cargo to South Carolina, while he was actually sailing to Lisbon.

Phillips decided this situation matched the issues raised by Vice-Admiral Sawyer previously. Namely that he should assist any American shipping endeavoring to deliver supplies to Wellington and his Army. Accordingly, he told the merchant captain he considered it his duty to escort the pair to the continent. He warned them if they should attempt to make for a French controlled port, they would immediately be taken as prizes.

More American ships were seen in succeeding days, but they all sailed well clear of Andromeda and her little convoy. Phillips suspected at least some of them were on similar missions as his own little flock, but he could not approach them without abandoning these two ships, so he allowed them to go un-molested. Off the mouth of the Tagus River, he left his charges to their own devices and spoke HMS Pelorus, brig-sloop of 18 guns, commanded by Captain Rowley, on her way to the Med.

Explaining his intelligence for the enemy privateers believed to be in the vicinity, he was assured the message would be relayed at Gibraltar. Continuing alone on her way toward the Channel, Andromeda met with a broken-winged brigantine sailing out to sea. She had evidently been in an action. Patched shot scars showed in her hull and her mainsail gaff had been shot away. An inadequate looking temporary spar had been hastily rigged, but Phillips did not expect her to carry her main very long in any kind of weather.

Andromeda ran her down, and she proved to be a British vessel taken two days before. Her American prize crew were now searching for a French port she could take refuge in. Re-captured without a struggle, her British crew was still aboard. They gave their information to their rescuers and it was learned a single American schooner had nabbed them. Releasing the brigantine to resume her voyage, Andromeda continued the hunt.

After entering the Channel, Cherbourg was off to starboard. It had been a rainy night and visibility was still poor the next morning. About three bells into the forenoon watch, muted gunfire was heard. There was disagreement on the quarterdeck as to just where the sound was coming from. With differing opinions expressed, Phillips turned to one of the helmsmen at his post.

Joshua Atkins had the reputation of having the best hearing on the ship, Phillips asked him if he had an idea of the bearing of the gunfire. Atkins was astonished at being asked, but confidently assured his captain the fire was coming from a few points to port. With no better advice, the captain told the helmsmen to steer on that bearing.

The gunfire had long been stopped when they discovered their quarry. The schooners they were looking for had taken on an unlikely opponent. The British flagged General Cornwallis, a former collier, had been armed with some twenty four pounder carronades and a pair of long sixes and went to sea with a letter of marque.

Mistaking her for an unarmed merchant ship in the haze, the schooners attacked. Normally, the target would have preferred to evade without action, to avoid expensive damage. However, the tubby former collier was unable to escape the lean schooners, so she put her topsails to the mast and prepared herself for action.

As soon as the predators felt the blows of those twenty four pound balls smashing into their thin scantlings, they knew they had a tiger by the tail. Had there only been one opponent, the British ship would have pounded that one to matchwood with her powerful guns, but there were two. One managed to get on Cornwallis' quarter and hammer her while the former collier was meting out punishment to the other schooner.

In the end, it was gunnery training that mattered. The American privateers, in their lengthy voyage, had managed to work up their crews to be more proficient than their opponent. All three vessels were to all intents and purposes destroyed in the melee, but it was the Cornwallis that pulled down her flag.

When Andromeda closed them, privateer crewmen were climbing around in the wreckage, attempting to find material that could be used to make one ship seaworthy. The post ship just ghosted up to the wreckage and fired a gun. The privateer's men, seeing an intact warship abeam with her guns run out, decided wisely to give it up. Now, it was Andromeda's men who began scrambling over the wrecks. Some of the first ones boarding a sinking schooner heard cries coming from her interior.

A slight pale figure emerged when freed. At first it appeared to be a young lad, but it soon was apparent the person, clad in overly large men's work clothing was female. Brought aboard Andromeda and introduced to Captain Phillips she was, it seemed, the woman taken captive weeks ago from the convoy off Bermuda. This was Anne Humphries, a rather plain young woman of maybe twenty years of age. To Phillips eye however, in her masculine garb she more resembled a fourteen year old lad.

He took the time to briefly question her before turning to the myriad tasks waiting his attention. Her paleness was explained by her account of being locked in the schooner's cramped lazarette for days at a time. Phillips was agreeably surprised by her fortitude. It must have been a harrowing ordeal being a prisoner of what were in effect a band of pirates, while dealing with the violent death of her father. However the woman displayed perfect calmness, asking only if she could be furnished a pan of fresh water and a bit of soap to wash up.

He ordered his servant to take her into his cabin and make her as comfortable as he could. In the meantime, he had a hundred enemy privateersmen to take in hand. That same number had gone over the side, and many more were suffering serious wounds, but he still had to find some means to secure these more-or-less able bodied men.

The British letter of marque was about to go down, pulled by the weight of her armament. One of the schooners was in similar condition, and Phillips would not have wagered she would stay above the waves another hour. The second schooner however, seemed in a little better condition, and Phillips ordered all hands, both British and American, to concentrate at emergency repairs to that schooner. The only effort expended on the two discarded ships was the work necessary to strip off any material likely to be needed to repair the survivor.

Despite a careful watch kept for friendly shipping in this well-travelled seaway, nothing was seen, and soon the two condemned ships went to the bottom. The third was saved at the last minute when effective patches was finally fitted to the shot holes below the waterline in her hull.

When most of the water was finally pumped out the next day, all of the healthy prisoners were battened in her hold, after anything usable as a weapon was removed. Jury masts and rigging were set up and a well-armed prize crew were put aboard to take her into Plymouth.

Phillips knew she would bring nothing worthwhile for them as a prize. She was good for nothing now except to be broken up for firewood. However, Andromeda's crew would earn a few hundred pounds head money for the surrendered prisoners. Before the schooner departed, Phillips asked Anne if she would wish to sail into Plymouth in her. She could be in civilized surroundings within two days.

She demurred however. She had no family left, and her captors had stripped her of all the funds she had in the world. She needed to get to Trinidad, where she thought an uncle was stationed in the Forces. Besides, this schooner was the one she had been captive in so long. She wished nothing more to do with it.

Phillips assured her she was welcome to stay on the Andromeda as long as they remained at sea, but sooner or later, he would be compelled to report back to Admiral Sawyer in Halifax. By rights he should report here at Plymouth, but had decided not to. He was still covered by the orders he had received from Sawyer and wished to continue his search for privateers.

Putting Acting Lieutenant Otis in charge of the schooner, he entrusted him with his accumulated reports, especially the details of activities of the newly taken privateers. Bidding Otis goodbye, the two vessels parted.

The schooner set out on its short dash into Plymouth, while Phillips was going back out into the Atlantic to see what he could discover of more privateer activity.

CHAPTER THIRTEEN

The weather turned foul, eventually requiring them to run before the wind showing just a scrap of fore staysail and a corner of the fore tops'l. It was necessary to stay ahead of the following seas, to prevent a wave from coming over the stern and causing, perhaps, irreparable damage. With the ship shut up tight, and the proper speed maintained this problem was minimized.

Another difficulty was the strain being placed on the rigging, especially the shrouds and stays that kept the masts upright. Tremendous forces were involved, and the cordage could stretch or otherwise fail.

The bosun and his mates were kept busy in the storm, making sure all was secure, as were indeed the gunner and his mates also. Disaster could ensue should one of the guns break loose and go careening around the deck or through the side of the ship.

Phillips had intended to have the carpenter put up an extra bulkhead in his cabin and construct a bed for his passenger. To his surprise, Anne was not the least bit discommoded by the weather and whenever she could get the officer of the watch to agree, took station on the quarterdeck, as if she were one of the officers. With the carpenter being too busy taking care of incessant ship emergencies to make the planned alterations to the captain's quarters, Anne begged to be allowed to take over the absent third officer's tiny cabin in the wardroom.

By the time the storm had ran its course, Anne had become accepted as one of the regulars on the quarterdeck. On the first day conditions allowed the officers to take their noon sights, Mister Darby offered to show her how to use his sextant. She replied with a laugh. "Lord, Mister Darby, I have been using a sextant since I was ten. Many a time I took the deck of my father's brig when he had taken aboard too much rum the night before."

Gradually, the young woman took on more of the duties ordinarily given to one of the midshipmen or junior lieutenants. This was welcomed by Phillips, since with the departure of Mister Otis, he did not really have a midshipman to whom he felt he could safely entrust the ship.

While Anne had never experienced any training in purely naval affairs, she was as capable as any of the other officers in the day to day operation of the ship. The only difficulty was, in her previous experience, she had only a few seamen in her charge. Now, with well over a hundred men to control, matters were very different.

With just himself, Gould, Darby and the sailing master capable of handling the ship, there was little rest for any of them. Anne, however, was knowledgeable and was able to convince Phillips of her ability to take the deck when needed. The major problem that presented itself concerned the crew. Some of the seamen could well baulk at an important moment when taking an order from the slightly build young woman.

Thinking about the matter, with his own rest and that of his officers in mind, Phillips realized how much simpler it would be if Anne could take an occasional watch, when other difficulties intruded. An idea came to him as he watched a seaman, Thomas Lane directing a party who were taking down the old fore topsail and hoisting aloft the new.

Lane was an old seaman, perhaps too old for his duties, maybe forty years of age or more. He was a massively built man, and few sane people would offer to take issue with him for any reason. Perfectly comfortable for any duties involved with seamanship itself, Lane was illiterate and barely able to count much past ten. But, when he gave an order, all men addressed took heed.

Anne was standing by the helm when the idea came to him. As soon as Lane's crew finished their task, Phillips called him aft. Lane, as well as most of the others in the crew, had always been perfectly respectful of the woman. When Lane approached, touching his brow to his captain and Miss Humphries, Phillips said his piece.

"Miss Humphries, Mister Lane, it seems I have a difficulty with which I would ask your assistance. As you know, with the departure of Mister Otis, we are short of a deck officer. Miss Humphries impresses me as a person who is well skilled in ship handling and navigation. Of course, as a civilian, the Navy would take me to task should I put her in charge of the deck. And, the question I have, is whether all the hands would obey her orders?"

"The thought occurs to me, I could put both of you, Miss Humphries, and you, Mister Lane, together in charge of the deck when needed. Miss Lane would make such decisions as ship handling and whatever navigational problems may arise on your watch. Mister Lane, your assistance here will be as a petty officer, ensuring the ready obedience of orders Miss Humphries gives. Should any crew members object to her orders, it will be your task to convince them to obey."

A dour Mister Gould found it difficult to agree with all of these changes. As he assured his fellow officers, nothing good would come of this woman aboard ship, especially one ensconced in the previously all-male wardroom. He was convinced the woman should have been sent into Plymouth with the schooner. How in the devil were they to be able to cater to all of her feminine whims and demands?

As the presiding officer of the mess, he was able to hold forth at every meal with his theories, some of them close to mutinous. The younger officers found such talk difficult to listen to, but felt unable to respond.

There turned out to be few problems. At first, there were those men who objected to following the orders of a young woman. Petty Officer Lane very forcefully informed those it would not be politic if they refused. In any event, Anne made it easy for the men to follow her directions. Whenever possible, she attempted to ask the men respectfully if they would set to some task. At first, there were those who tried to confuse her with questions of sometimes arcane topics, but she eventually convinced most of them of her knowledge of seamanship.

In any event, there were few men aboard Andromeda who found it difficult to follow the requests of a charming woman. Phillips was impressed with her ability to have the men follow her orders without raising her voice.

By the time they were approaching the midway point in the crossing, although Mister Gould remained as dour as ever, all else had become used to the new order. Anne was just as effective in her duties as any of the other officers and Phillips found himself regretting the moment when he would need to put her ashore.

At this time, they met up with an old acquaintance. The merchant ship Rebecca Morris they had met on the outward voyage, when she was carrying wheat and spars to the port of Lisbon. Here she was again, still deeply laden, and struggling west with visible damage aloft. The masthead lookout reported her ahead while she was still hull-down and Andromeda caught up with the slow moving merchant just before dark. Coming along side, she was questioned about her difficulty. She replied she had been caught up in a storm, and had some of her canvas carry away.

When Phillips asked if he could be of assistance, her captain declined. Asked her current cargo, she replied she was carrying lemons to Boston. Now, this was a perfectly innocuous cargo, which Phillips was inclined to let pass, in view of her previous service of delivering badly needed wheat to Wellington's forces on the Peninsula. He did wonder why such a cargo, since citrus was readily available in the Caribbean, much closer to home and with less danger of spoilage.

However, he was prepared to believe this was the only cargo the ship could take aboard that would not meet with the displeasure of British blockaders.

Phillips was tempted to send over a party to rummage the hold to inspect for anything illicit. But, he reasoned it would have been difficult to take such aboard in Lisbon, and with the ill-feeling between the two countries that had brought about this new war, he was reluctant to do anything to inflame the situation any more than necessary.

The two ships parted company and proceeded on their separate ways. During the night another storm brewed up, and Phillips remained on deck all night. A sudden squall almost took the ship aback, but some skilled work by the watch on deck and Mister Darby brought her through. At first light next morning, a calmer sea revealed the Rebecca Morris far behind them, and she appeared to be in a strange state.

Andromeda was put about, since the merchant ship seemed to have lost most of her canvas during the night, with her main topmast as well. She had also acquired a severe list that put her lee rail in the sea and threatened to send her sticks over the side. Working her way back to the merchant, it was late in the forenoon watch before they came up alongside. Little had been done to right the ship, but she looked to Phillips to be in serious straits indeed.

Taking Anne with him in the launch, Phillips was pulled over to examine the situation at first hand. Few men were on deck and the mate of the watch was reluctant to allow them to board. Phillips offered to return to Andromeda and return with an armed boarding party.

With that, lines were lowered and the party boarded. It was soon discovered the ship had been overcome with a huge wave sweeping up over her stern in the blow. Many of her crew on deck, as well as the captain, had been swept overboard and lost. The few men remaining were doing what they could, but it was little enough.

A foremast staysail had been set and this was pulling the ship westward, but the lee rail was perilously close to the water because of her list. Phillips was well aware this was a ship under an enemy flag, and something was wrong. He asked Anne if she would return to Andromeda and bring back an armed party.

On her return, she asked if she could take some men below to inspect the cargo. She assured Phillips she was knowledgeable about its proper stowage, and might be able to determine the problem. She suspected the contents of the hold had shifted during the storm, and hoped she could determine how to correct the problem.

Phillips himself was not familiar with the proper stowage of a hold. In his experience, it had always been the sailing master who handled that task. Anne was below almost an hour while the Andromeda's men were hoisting some canvas brought over from Andromeda, and seeing to the standing rigging.

A stern-faced, Anne Humphries, came on deck and delivered her summation. "The cargo did shift during the blow, but it was not the lemons that did it. There is a cargo of big guns low down in the hold, and over that, cases of muskets in crates. That is what shifted. They had a few tons of lemons on top of the weapons to hide them from casual view."

Immediately, Phillips went below to inspect for himself. The guns, he was able to examine, each had the Imperial $\mathscr{N}$ cast into the breech. The muskets were all of

French military issue. He ordered the merchant's crew to be taken in custody, and he informed the mate in command the ship was now a prize of the Royal Navy.

Phillips attempted to learn from the crew of the merchantman where the cargo had been taken on board. At first, no one would talk, but soon Anne came to him. Before the American crew was arrested, she had worked alongside them. Afterward, she informed Phillips one had come to her with a story.

The fellow claimed to be a former Royal Navy crewman discharged from Indefatigable years ago who then emigrated to America. He had once served as a crewman aboard a hulk in the Thames and did not wish to go back to one as a prisoner of war. He offered to tell all if he were given leniency.

Phillips let the matter ride while they were getting the merchantman seaworthy again. Her hold had to be opened and the cargo hoisted up and later re-stowed. The loose fruit was simply thrown over the side. Once they were able to bring up the crates of muskets, they were then able to get at the guns. Phillips would have liked to drop them over the side also, but they would be evidence. So they were re-stowed, and wedged into place with whatever came to hand. Eventually, some of the musket crates were found to be broken, so individual muskets were used for dunnage.

Fortunately, the weather remained fairly reasonable for that day and the next when the ship was finally riding on an even keel. Some of the old canvas Andromeda had used as a disguise, was sent aboard and sail was got on the ship.

Now was the time to deal with their potential informer. The fellow was brought up from the orlop deck where he had been in chains for the past few days. Considering the fellow to be in the proper frame of mind now, Phillips ordered him brought aft.

CHAPTER FOURTEEN

Bob Laskins was a pitiful looking specimen when he was brought before Phillips. Nearly toothless his hair was long and unkempt, down below his shoulders. Having been in irons, he had been unable to braid his queue. His stench was overpowering. Phillips had ordered Mister Gould to sit there in the cabin with him. One look at Gould's face might easily influence a man to think he was about to be sent to the Inquisition.

The questioning at first was light. Laskins was not the brightest man on the ship, and his questioners were soon able to determine when he was telling lies, which was most of the time. He claimed to have been discharged from Indefatigable before the present war, but he inadvertently revealed he had served on Niobe since then. It was likely Laskins was a runner.

With all of this out of the way, Phillips asked the man straight out where the merchant had loaded the arms. Laskins wanted Phillips to promise he would be released upon reaching shore, without being sent to a prison hulk.

Phillips turned to Gould, who had already been told what he should tell the man. Phillips thought Gould could do a better job of frightening the man than he could do himself.

Gould glared at the seaman. "Laskins, so far you have told us a parcel of lies. From your own mouth, you have incriminated yourself as a deserter. Spending the next few years in a prison hulk is the least of your worries. What you have to worry about first is whether you will have the flesh flogged from your back as a deserter, or whether you will be merely hung up as serving aboard an enemy ship against your own country."

Gibbering with fear, Laskins swore he would tell the truth if only his life would be spared. Facing Gould's glare, finally Laskins surrendered. It seemed after unloading her cargo in Lisbon, the ship had taken aboard a cargo of raw wool supposedly bound for Boston. In view of her service in bringing supplies to Wellington, the ship was granted a license to satisfy any blockading ships that might stop her.

Leaving Lisbon, she had sailed northerly up the Iberian Peninsula then eastward to the French port of Bayonne. She dodged the watchdog frigate there and made her way into the port. There, she sold her wool and purchased the weapons to deliver to the United States. These, were of course, prohibited contraband, and were concealed under a mass of loose lemons. The ship then set out for Boston, sailing in the midst of a blow that drove the blockading ships out to sea.

Gould pounced on him. "You tell us the ship carried a British license to carry raw wool to the States. Where did she get the license saying she was laden with lemons?"

The stricken seaman fearfully stammered that he did not know. "The captain and first mate handled all of that and the crew was never told."

103

With a glance at Gould, Phillips iterated that statement was probably true. "I expect the French authorities have someone who can copy our own licenses with a fair degree of accuracy." With a final glance at Laskins, Phillips assured him he would not go to a prison hulk. Instead he would be allowed to sign on to Andromeda as a crewman, with a warning.

"Should you attempt to desert again, I can promise you a fast court martial and a flogging around the fleet. Govern yourself accordingly."

The pair sailed westward in company, Darby commanding the prize. Andromeda still was resembling a dowdy merchant with her drab paint. Hoping for yet another privateer, Phillips sailed the line of latitude leading to Halifax. This far along on their voyage, many ships without an accurate chronometer often sailed such a line to port, since it was much easier to determine their latitude than the proper longitude. Therefore, a ship could be sailed right along that line until land was sighted.

Of course, enemy predators also knew this, and it was not unusual for a warship to station herself on that line and wait until a fat prize sailed into her clutches. From a distance, Andromeda and her consort appeared to be just that, a pair of merchantmen who had somehow become separated from their convoy, making for the British port of Halifax by the most direct means.

To the General Washington, an American privateer brig of twelve guns, the only question was whether both ships could be harvested at the same time. Should they separate, it might be difficult. Some caution was evidenced at first, but it was soon decided the pair of plain ships were clearly merchantmen, with no capacity to do the privateer any harm.

To the temporary relief of Captain Ezra Benson of the Washington, they did not separate. He suspected the individual ship captains thought together they could fight him off. He had a well drilled crew and a large number of boarders aboard.

With a fast ship and few British warships abroad yet on blockade duty, he planned to be out for not over a week at a time, allowing him to sail with a large crew aboard without the necessity to concern himself much about provisions. Hopefully, any prospective prize could be taken by swarming aboard a large number of boarders with the objective of capturing the prize with minimal damage.

On board Andromeda, the stranger was immediately identified to be a likely privateer. There were still many miles of separation between the privateer and its intended prey, so Phillips hurriedly scrawled out instructions to the Morris, and asked Anne to jump down into the jolly boat and deliver them to Mister Darby.

Darby was simply instructed to follow in Andromeda's wake and follow her lead. When Andromeda hoisted her flag, the Morris was to hoist the British ensign over the American. This would indicate she was a prize to the British warship. She must not give that notice however, until so ordered. When Anne returned from her mission, Phillips told her to go below before the expected action commenced. "If you desire to be useful, you can assist the doctor" Phillips suggested.

"Sir", she replied. "You have few enough officers for the deck. I will admit that I know nothing about gunnery and fighting, but I do know how to sail and command a ship. If you would permit, I could take the place of Mister Harding, the sailing master. I am sure he could prove useful on your guns."

Phillips explained to her the savagery of ship-board combat and the blood and the terrible wounds that would be expected. When she refused to withdraw her offer though, Phillips, with some reservations, decided to allow her to perform Mister Harding's duties with his consent.

Harding himself had his own reservations, but agreed, since he would be commanding a section of the guns he would be on deck and could step into the breach, if she faltered.

On Phillip's order, Anne had the courses furled, the ship proceeding under her tops'ls. This accomplished two purposes. Getting those big sails that were low to the deck and close to the big guns firing out of the way, eliminated a fire hazard. For another, the speed of Andromeda through the water was reduced, giving her captain more time to make decisions.

The captain of the oncoming brig saw no need to procrastinate. He bore right in toward, what he imagined to be the leading merchantman. The brig was coming toward Andromeda's starboard beam and obviously planned to run alongside her and use his numerous crew to swarm aboard. As a warning though, the privateer first fired a bowchaser. The six pound ball just nicked the starboard bow, barely penetrating Andromeda's tough oak.

Phillips decided this was close enough and had Anne bring the ship around. She had the helm put over and flatted the jib to bring her head around. As the ship turned in front of the brig, Phillips ordered the guns run out.

There was no instantaneous discharge of the guns. Each gun captain had been instructed to fire only when he was sure of a hit. Mister Harding walked in the rear of the broadside guns, from bow to stern. He did not actually interfere, but observed the gun captains taking careful aim, perhaps calling for a gun to be shifted from one side or another or ordering the quoin's position under the breech moved in or out, changing the elevation of the gun. The guns fired in singles and pairs, at a close enough range that no misses were observed.

The brig was in trouble. While a few of her crew had served in warships before, more had not. At the time she fitted out, most of the experienced seamen available who had actually previously fought in an action, had already signed aboard another privateer or had gone aboard one of the ships of the regular US Navy. Many of the crew were either peacetime seamen or casual laborers signed on as boarders who had absolutely no experience with being under fire from big guns.

When the re-loaded guns began vomiting out their deadly charges of those little iron plums, many of these men broke and began running for the hatches, hoping to escape the carnage on deck. The enemy captain roared at his people, attempting to make them return to their duty of bringing the brig around so she might possibly make her escape.

However, the same charge of grape that laid the other quarterdeck officers low, struck the captain. One of those iron plums half severed his neck, putting an end of his shouting.

One of the privateer's hands slashed a halyard with his knife and the flag came fluttering down.

Phillips now had a dilemma. He had another prize and it was not too badly damaged. What he did not have was a surplus of officers. His only remaining deck officers were the sailing master and Mister Gould, the first officer. To tell the truth, he did not altogether trust that man out of his sight. Gould's main tools for obtaining obedience were shouts and threats.

Phillips knew he would have to be concerned that Gould, if placed in command of the new prize, might soon find himself tipped overboard one night and the prize sailed off to Boston by a mutinous crew.

He could, of course, put the sailing master in charge of the prize, but he still needed someone he had absolute confidence aboard the post ship to second himself.

Anne would just have to step into the breach again. While the Navy would never countenance putting a woman in command of a prize, there would be no quibble if an experienced petty officer were so placed. Besides, he trusted the woman. Calling Humphries and Lane aft, he explained his thinking.

Lane was aghast that he was being placed in command of a ship, but Anne explained. "The Navy will never let a woman serve as captain, but you can. I will make the decisions, you just see that they are carried out." With Lane's fears settled, the pair joined the boarding party on the captive brig and began putting the brig back together.

While there had been many casualties aboard the brig, there were still many healthy men, perfectly capable of rising up some night and taking the brig back. Searching the former privateer, a party located a dozen swivel guns. These were large bore guns, something like a huge shotgun. A pintle was fastened underneath the weapon allowing it to be fired from a steady rest.

With so many prisoners to guard, it was decided to remove anything below deck that could possibly be used as a weapon and just batten the hatches with the prisoners below.

One of the brig's guns was a little four pounder, and that was mounted right aft, covering the hatch openings. The swivel guns were mounted wherever a spot could be found. Two were placed up in the maintop so as to cover the deck below. There were several charges of case shot aboard, basically thin metal canisters filled with pistol balls. One of those charges was broken open and the swivels loaded with their shot.

The senior officer of the captured brig Phillips thought was too capable to leave aboard the vessel, so this officer came onto Andromeda, and was ensconced in the wardroom, with a Marine standing guard. Several of the privateer petty officers were shown some of the weapons before being locked below to witness what they could expect if they broke free. Before Phillips gave Anne the necessary pages copied from the signal book, he handed her the pair of pistols he had purchased the last time he was ashore in Halifax. He demonstrated the use of the new ignition system and explained the advantages. He insisted Anne keep an eye open for trouble and meet any with a firm hand.

The prize crew of the brig would have to sleep rough on deck for the next few days until they made port. The only people below deck were the captives.

The three vessels were proceeding on course for Halifax. At two bells of the morning watch Chips, standing a deck watch, noted in his log he had heard what sounded like two pistol shots aboard the latest prize, followed closely by the reports of larger guns. The post ship was leading the Washington by a good cable's length. Chips put the ship about and called for Phillips. Andromeda was shortly hove-to off the bow of the brig with her guns run out. Phillips filled the launch with Marines and accompanied them aboard the Washington.

Anne met them at the entry port. All was peaceful now. Some of the prisoners had found an overlooked gun crow below and used it to pry the patch from a shot hole in the brig's starboard beam. The watch on deck was alerted by the splash when the material fell into the sea. Anne went to the rail with her pistols and fired at the two men that emerged.

Simultaneously, the prisoners below were using that same crow to pry loose a hatch. It had just been opened enough for a man to scramble through when both swivel guns in the tops fired. With each guns loaded with a dozen half inch pistol balls, fearful execution was done on the people below decks. The small balls penetrated the deck planking and struck whomever was below. Phillips had the hatch removed and ordered the wounded men pulled out. With this done, the hatch was secured again and the wounded sent to Andromeda for treatment. The pair of men Anne had fired upon were never seen again. They had fallen into the sea and were lost.

It was an anti-climactic moment when Andromeda fired off the salute to Admiral Sawyer's flag and picked up her mooring. The pilot aboard the Washington, took her to the other side of the harbor and that was the last Phillips saw of Anne for the next few days. The Morris also anchored in the commercial anchorage, and early on Mister Darby, replaced by an official from the prize court, was returned to Andromeda.

Mister Gould had previously asked to go ashore on some private business and Phillips was glad to oblige him. In recent days it was becoming ever more difficult to exist on the same ship with the dour first officer.

After two days, Gould had not returned and then a smartly uniformed midshipman delivered a note from Admiral Sawyer. Phillips was invited to Sawyer's house ashore for dinner and to bring the admiral up to date of his activities since leaving port earlier in the summer.

As Phillips was led by the admiral's man past a little anteroom, he saw Lieutenant Gould seated at a little table, a massive pile of paper before him. Gould saw him but spoke not a word. With some misgivings, Phillips went into the Admiral's working office where a light repast had been laid out on a side board. When Phillips straightened to report, Sawyer waved him off.

"Let us dispense with formality for a while, lad. I just want to hear what you have been up to from your own mouth."

Phillips had his records and log with him but the Admiral just wanted a vocal report. He spent the next two hours going over the events of the summer since he had left port. When he finished, Sawyer told him he had learned of some of these activities before. A packet from England had arrived the week before with copies of the reports Phillips had sent ashore to Plymouth.

"Let me tell you Captain. The Plymouth port admiral is very displeased with you for not reporting to him when you were just offshore. I will try to cover over the situation just in case you ever happen to serve under the fellow in the future. We were mids together a half century ago, and he was always a touchy sort.'

"Now, I want you to tell me about the orgies that took place in your cabin and the wardroom on your ship."

"Orgies, Sir? I hardly know how to answer you. There were no orgies on my ship. Nor was there anyone to have an orgy with, to make the answer more clear."

"That is too bad Captain. I had thought to be entertained by a good story of your misdeeds. I hear that a ravishing beauty has bewitched the officers on Andromeda, especially yourself. The story was she kept you all very busy, morning and night."

A red veil of rage swept over Phillips vision. "Admiral Sawyer, I must ask you to tell me who reported such nonsense. A fine woman's name is being besmirched and I find it necessary to call the culprit out. I realize this is contrary to present Navy rules, so I am taking this opportunity to offer my resignation."

"Calm down, Captain. For one thing, I can't afford to lose you. For another, I have talked to Miss Humphries herself and the teller of tales is now a laughing stock on this station. A seaman I sailed with many years ago accompanied her, Lane his name was. I had nearly forgotten it but it popped out as soon as I saw his face."

"She seems to be quite a prodigy herself. At least Lane thinks so. I hear tell you put her in command of that last privateer brig you brought in. Lane told me she pistoled two men that escaped from below and tried to take over the ship."

"I am going to first ask you and then to order you to let this matter lie. I have the man serving in my outer office where he can do no harm. I aim to send him back home soon with his records flagged to insure he never goes to sea as an officer again."

"We are talking about Lieutenant Gould here, Admiral Sawyer?"

"You said it, not me Phillips. Now that is the end of it. I have another officer on my establishment who has been annoying me daily with requests to go to sea. I expect you will find him aboard your ship when you return."

"Now, on to more pleasant subjects, Captain. That Miss Humphries is a very fortunate young woman."

"Why so, Sir?"

"Well, the merchantman her father owned was covered by insurance. The salvage costs will be fully covered, so the young woman now owns her trading brig free and clear.

Her captain is still here in Halifax and has engaged a crew. The lady will be able to sail as soon as she can obtain a cargo."

CHAPTER FIFTEEN

Anne was pulled out to Andromeda in the boat from her own merchant brig, the Sarah Hayes, which she had recently re-claimed from the prize court. There had been a question of ownership, but with a will located giving her all of her father's assets, the question was resolved. With that settled, she gave the command to her previous captain and moved back into her old cabin. She brought her thanks and the pistols he had loaned her. He wondered if she was going to sail to Trinidad to find her uncle, but she thought not.

"I found a warehouse full of American grain that was looking for a ship to take it to England. HMS Ajax brought in an American prize last month loaded with wheat. I was there yesterday when it was offered up for sale and I purchased the lot. A convoy leaves next week for home and I plan to be in it. Grain prices are very high in Britain what with the harvest problems and I hope to make a little money with this cargo. I do not wish to appear on my uncle's doorstep as a supplicant, so will likely wait until I have become more substantial before calling on him."

They spent an hour reminiscing their adventures that summer, then it was time for her to leave. Not a single word was said about the spurious allegations of Mister Gould.

In due course, a shabby shipyard barge arrived alongside Andromeda and disgorged a well-built young lieutenant as well as a master's mate in his mid-twenties. Lieutenant Hornady introduced Mister Wilson to Phillips as he handed over their orders.

"Sir, I am most dreadfully sorry to be late in reporting. However, I had to drop by the pawn-broker to retrieve my sextant. There, I met Mister Wilson here who begged me to allow him to accompany me in the dockyard boat, funds being rather low."

Phillips called Mister Darby up from the wardroom and introduced him to the newcomers. There was some delicate probing between the two lieutenants to determine each other's date of commission, since this would determine which one was senior. It was soon determined Hornady was senior by a matter of a few months, so he was now the ships first officer. Darby was second and Phillips offered Wilson a temporary lieutenant's position as third officer. Wilson had passed his board a year ago but was never made, so there was now a good chance Admiral Sawyer might confirm the appointment.

At present, there were the thousand tasks needed to be taken care of to get the ship ready to return to sea. Hornady's last position had been in the Admiral's office and he was able to confirm to Phillips the Admiral was in the process of generating orders to send them back out again.

Andromeda's larder had been nearly emptied on her last cruise so now tons of biscuit had to be brought on board, as well as barrels of salted beef and pork, newly smuggled up the coast from Massachusetts.

Much of the beef, as well as the flour used to make the biscuit Phillips learned, was regularly brought up from the United States by schooner. Nationalities be damned, the shrewd Yankee traders were still doing business with old customers, never mind what flag they sailed under.

The last of the water came aboard and now the ship was ready to sail, just as soon as the order came. The papers were delivered aboard one dismal, rainy morning. They seemed simple enough. He was to proceed to sea, being careful to avoid enemy warships superior to Andromeda and harry American and French commerce. Prizes taken should be sent to the nearest British port if possible, otherwise they were to be destroyed.

Phillips was notified of the blockade that had been imposed upon major American ports, and was required to cooperate with any of said blockading ships that needed his assistance. He was warned that several powerfully built American frigates were at sea, and he should avoid action with the larger of the enemy warships, but should report their locations to any available warships of the Royal Navy.

Making her way out to sea, Andromeda spent the next few days shaking down. Many new hands had been brought aboard and they had to be integrated with the seasoned men. Some of the hand's mess tables had new

117

members added, and there was initial suspicion and controversy at first. Eventually, after some shifting around, matters were organized to the hand's satisfaction.

On the first fine day after leaving port, Phillips spoke to both watches separately, before and after the noon watch change. He was mainly addressing the newcomers, but was also reminding the oldsters of how he wanted matters handled.

He was able to report the earnings made by an average able seaman from prize money on the past voyage. He assured the men this sum, equal to a year's pay in itself, could easily be increased this voyage.

"On our last voyage, we were required to find and take as many enemy privateers as possible. These ships ordinarily will not fetch nearly the sum a well-laden merchant will bring. While we are still to do that, we are also tasked with disrupting the enemy's commerce, whenever we can. This means, we are free to take as many prizes as possible.

I must warn you, of course, while we will send as many prizes back to port as we can, there will come a time when we will not be able to spare crews for some of the ships. At that time, it may be necessary to burn some of the lower value prizes. I want to hear no grumbling from you when this is done. Are we clear?"

Once out in the shipping lanes, merchantmen began to be encountered, sailing under several flags. French-flagged vessels were almost non-existent here, so Andromeda was concerned about Americans. As before, American flagged vessels were to be examined closely to make sure of their destination. Most Americans encountered could be assumed to be fair prizes, but there were still a few carrying important cargo bound for British controlled ports that should be left to proceed.

Those vessels carrying trade for non-British destinations were immediately collected and sent back to port with a prize crew commanded by a senior midshipman. Admiral Sawyer had furnished Andromeda with several, after Phillips explained his problems with furnishing prize masters from his own resources. Some of these individuals were locals with previous experience in the mercantile trade. Mister Harding immediately set to, instructing the new mids with what they would need to know as commanders of their own vessels.

At the moment, Jonathon Benson was on the quarterdeck beside him, chiefly to learn what he could, and to relay orders and messages to their proper recipients. Many of the new mids Phillips had previously come into contact with were mere children. These latter were often men in their twenties, some of whom had been commanding fishing boats and small traders for years. Benson here had last served aboard a trader delivering illicit cargo out of ports in Maine up to Halifax. Some of that cargo would probably be aboard the next convoy to Britain.

Phillips, having a quiet spell, with nothing demanding his immediate attention, took the opportunity to question the mid about his motives for entering the Service.

"Mister Benson, just what do you hope to gain from the Royal Navy in your service with us?"

"Sir, I realize I am too old to ever be able to make a career out of the Navy. I had originally expected to take

119

over my father's schooner when he gave up the sea. She was taken however, on a trip up from Salem, last month, and that hope is gone. I have been sailing on other smuggling vessels to keep myself alive, but know I will soon join my father in captivity, if I keep doing this."

"My mother met Admiral Sawyer last month at a soiree and asked him if there was no place for me in the Royal Navy. The call came just before you sailed, and that is why I am here. I hope to be able to make a living until the war is over, then perhaps I can get back to sailing for myself."

Phillips stood quietly for some minutes mulling over what Harrison had told him. Then, he replied. "Mister Benson, you will understand most young men come to us as children, their parents expecting us to train the young lads into promising officers. Very often, that does not happen. Either they have no aptitude for it, or they may be knocked in the head before they become old enough."

"If a lad does live until he is sixteen or so, we will probably find out whether he has learned what he needs to know as a potential officer. I asked Admiral Sawyer to supply me with young men I could use to command prizes we take back to port. You were one of the people he sent me. In the coming weeks, I may test your knowledge of ship handling, navigation and your ability to handle seamen."

"For now, from what I have seen, you appear to be much more useful than the average midshipman. You have probably come in contact with Mister Wilson, who came aboard as master's mate. Lacking a third lieutenant, I appointed him as acting third lieutenant, which leaves me without a master's mate. I will therefore appoint you to that position, temporarily. That means, if I choose, I may dis-rate you back to midshipman, or even seaman if I think it advisable. Should you succeed, there is no limit to how far you may advance, given a long war and plenty of prizes."

"Probably, if you can satisfy the officers appointed over you, you can expect to receive command of a future prize to take to port. For now, you will take charge of the midshipman aboard Andromeda. Mister Wilson has been handling that chore, and I wish to relieve him of the duty. You will do what you can to impart lessons of seamanship into the hard heads of the mids, and handle any minor disciplinary problems. Have you any questions?"

Andromeda ranged into the shipping lanes leading home. Now and again a ship was found to be a fair prize and she was manned and sent home. Mister Wilson had been given command of an American brigantine loaded with sawn timber destined for the shipbuilding trade in Bordeaux. Phillips had been amazed the owners would have tried to deliver the cargo to that port, rather than a port in Britain. However, the ways of ship-owners were not for him to determine. The cargo would end its journey in England, and Mister Wilson would have his opportunity to command a ship.

Continuing her sweep, Andromeda sighted a pair of ships together. A big, ship-rigged merchant was alongside a slim schooner. As the warship approached, the ship dis-engaged and tried to escape. The schooner lay there in the water, broadside to the swells. Her foremast had come down and was presently over the side. Ranging alongside, Andromeda fired a gun, the shot striking the water well clear of the stricken vessel. The schooner promptly struck his flag and Phillips sent Mister Bentley over in the longboat with a party of armed seamen. Bentley was one of the promising mids, only fifteen, but becoming useful on the ship.

Warning the master of the vessel by his speaking trumpet to mind his manners until his return, Phillips sailed on after the ship.

It took only a short time until the master of that ship realized he had no chance for escape. With Andromeda broadside to her a long musket range, she wisely backed her topsails and lowered her flag. This time Mister Benson was the one getting the nod to board the prize. After taking the necessary men, the crew left aboard Andromeda was getting rather sparse. Phillips stood by until Benson reported by speaking trumpet the prize was secure.

Phillips ordered him to get the ship on the wind and take her into Halifax, where he would be met. Now, Andromeda returned to the schooner, which seemed to be having some difficulties. The boarding party was congregated in the stern, and a crowd of shouting crew brandishing weapons to their front. Phillips was impressed to see the diminutive fifteen year old to the fore of his crew, with his dirk out. A petty officer behind the lad had his cutlass out, attempting to defend the lad.

A gun fired, halting the defiance and more men were taken over. When Mister Darby returned, he reported. "Well sir, she reported herself to be a simple fishing schooner, and she did have the proper gear aboard. However, she also had a pair of twelve pounder carronades on each beam, covered with fishing nets. She also has a cargo of raw sugar in barrels in her hold. When I demanded to see her papers, they were all reported thrown over the side. However, upon searching the master's cabin, I found a letter of marque in his desk. She had an overly large crew aboard for either a fishing vessel or a merchantman and I think she was out after prizes. "

"Apparently, she went after a British merchant that also had some carronades on board. It was a shot from that one that knocked her foremast down. When Mister Bentley went aboard, her own large crew came up on deck after we left and were attempting to resist capture."

Phillips thought about the matter. "So, we have a vessel with a cargo but with no manifest. It does have a pair of guns and a letter of marque. It seems we do have a legitimate prize. What about Bentley? Do you think he is capable of commanding a prize?"

"I do not see why not, Captain. It was only that he did not have a large enough boarding party to handle all those men on the schooner."

Phillips removed those people from the schooner that he could and confined them aboard Andromeda. Re-enforcing the prize crew, he ordered that foremast repaired and the vessel sailed into Halifax.

Andromeda remained near the schooner until she was able to get under way, then left to see to the other prize. Night fell before they reached the ship and they did not actually speak her until the next day. All was well, and the warship escorted her prize on the slow voyage toward Halifax. Toward evening, the schooner, much faster than the other two, caught up with them and all three entered port together.

CHAPTER SIXTEEN

With his prize crews back aboard and the ship re-supplied, Andromeda was ready to put back to sea again. He was well pleased with the activities of Mister Bentley and Mister Benson as prize masters. Both of these young gentlemen could be relied upon in the future. He brought the matter to Admiral Sawyer's attention while in harbor and Sawyer approved Mister Benson's appointment as Master's Mate.

On the forthcoming voyage, Phillips decided to venture out in the Atlantic, past the big Gulf current sweeping up past the continent and then sail south to Georgia. There was a British base at Pensacola where they could obtain necessary supplies if they wished to sail further south. From Georgia, he could follow the Gulf current up the American eastern seaboard and do what he could against any shipping.

The Andromeda made her way out to sea without incident and turned south. By this stage in the war, the British blockade was becoming firmly effective. There were some 'leakers' of fast, well-handled schooners, but it had become unprofitable to attempt trade with other American seaports, or those of Europe, unless one had a license from the admiral commanding the blockading fleet and was actually trading with England.

Resuming her disguise as a plodding merchant ship, Andromeda was investigated by several fast privateers, before one approached too closely. This one actually came up beam to beam with the post ship before she fired a gun. From a cable's length distance, Andromeda opened her ports, ran out her guns and waited. Phillips hoped the lightly built schooner would heave to and pull down her colors, but that was not to be.

Her out-witted captain fired her broadside guns and tried to bring the fast-handling vessel around to escape. This did not work out well for the privateer. Phillips reluctantly gave the order to fire as the little vessel presented her stern to the broadside.

At the close distance, nearly every shot struck, and her main fell forward, entangling itself in the rigging of the fore. More of the heavy caliber balls struck the counter and ranged forward, smashing men, guns and equipment as they went. The privateer halted, Andromeda sailed alongside, her guns reloaded and ready for any mischief. There was no offer of any at this stage, and the schooner lay hove-to peacefully as the boarding party went over.

Mister Harding went aboard the stricken vessel but returned, saying it would be doubtful if she could reach port. Even if she did, it would likely be more costly to repair her than buy a new schooner of similar size. In such circumstances, Phillips decided to destroy the vessel. He was not thrilled about putting the entire crew of the schooner on board Andromeda, but the schooner had only two boats surviving, both towing behind. There was insufficient capacity in the boats to take the entire crew.

In the end, the schooner's remaining boats were filled with as many of her crew as they could hold, provided with ship's biscuit, water and a chart and compass. The men were given a course to steer to reach port, and sent on their way. The remainder were placed up front in Andromeda's forecastle and guards placed on them to keep them from trouble. Slow match was laid to the powder magazine of the former privateer, then lit. An hour later, the crew of Andromeda watched the crippled vessel erupt in smoke and fire from a mile away.

With seventy angry men up in the bows of Andromeda, Phillips was not enthused about resuming his patrol with them aboard, so the ship closed on an off-shore island to the north of Philadelphia and put over a boat with an officer. Anchored in six fathoms, Phillips waited impatiently for the boat to return. On this coast, should the wind turn, the ship could find herself in serious trouble indeed. Every glass on the quarterdeck was trained on the shore party, and there was obvious relief when they returned to the boat and pulled back out.

Phillips waited on the quarterdeck until Mister Darby boarded. He reported the shore was deserted with no sign of immediate life, although there seemed to be a village of some sort to the south. If they landed the prisoners here, they should be able to reach help within a few hours.

Accordingly the prisoners were brought up from below and loaded into the launch, a boat load at a time. Before leaving, Phillips showed the captain of the former privateer a chart and the information of the village down the coast.

Each man before leaving the ship was allowed to drink as much water as he wished from the scuttle butt and given two ship's biscuits. As soon as the launch returned from delivering the last load of men, Andromeda pulled up her anchor and left.

This last capture had not been very profitable to them but at least they had removed another predator from the sea. Granted, they had returned the crew to their own country to resume their privateering, if that was their intention. Perhaps some of the actual seamen would indeed do that, but Phillips knew many, if not most, of the crew were laborers and landsmen, who had just been hoping to earn some easy money. The lesson they had just learned might show them there were easier wages that could be earned on land.

Proceeding to sea, Andromeda cruised off the coast for a few days without finding anything of note. Sailing eastward, then southerly, the main lookout spotted a sail farther out. As she closed on the sail, another came into view. Eventually the second sighting proved to be HMS Tenedos. Phillips ordered Andromeda's number flown. Tenedos had her number up as well as signal flags that could not be immediately read because of the distance.

The first sighting was a mystery however. Whatever it was it could be, it certainly was a big one. "Perhaps", Phillips reasoned, "it was an Indiaman."

Mister Wilson was the signal officer and Mister Bentley was his deputy. Both had young eyes and approached their captain, assuring him they had deciphered the signal from Tenedos. The signal was reported to be "Enemy in Sight'.

Andromeda repeated the signal. Then another was hoisted aboard Tenedos. 'Engage the Enemy'.

Acknowledging, the post ship beat to quarters and made for the enemy. As they closed, Mister Harding approached with his glass in his hand. "Sir", he reported.

I have seen that sail before in the Med. She is the United States frigate Constitution, likely a tough nut to crack."

"Well, Mister Harding, Tenedos is offshore of her and between the pair of us, I believe we can do our duty.

As Andromeda closed however, the wind began to drop, and it was seen Tenedos was having a difficult time closing the big enemy. Apparently she was in an area of light and fitful winds and was having trouble keeping her sails filled. The big American was having no such difficulty, perhaps because her tops were so much higher. She had set her royals and was making a wake.

With Tenedos now flying the signal, 'Engage the enemy more closely!' Phillips was in a quandary. The captain of Tenedos was senior to him and was well entitled to give him orders, especially in these circumstances. However, if there were to be any chance of victory in the forthcoming action, Tenedos would have to be involved. Andromeda could not hope to overcome the big American unless the thirty-eight gunned fifth rate could play a leading part. But, orders were orders.

Regardless of present circumstances, if he shied away from the action, he could expect to be hauled in front of a court on charges of cowardice, possibly losing his commission.

With guns run out, Andromeda continued her approach. At long gun range, she attempted to cross in front of Constitution, hoping to bow rake the huge ship. A successful shot just might possibly bring down some gear that might allow Tenedos to catch up. This did not happen. Phillips could see no results of their broadside, although one of the Constitution's bow guns placed a heavy ball through their lee beam, generating shouts from below as men were skewered with oaken splinters.

Deciding this was not the best way for him to fight the behemoth, he put his ship before the wind with Constitution chasing. This too had its dangers. With its taller sail plan, the enemy could get the stronger winds aloft, and even though massively heavier, could still outsail Andromeda.

At his wit's end, Phillips trained his glass on Tenedos, to see if she had any more orders. She did not, but at least was no longer telling him to close the enemy.

Dangerously close to Constitution, Phillips had a pair of twelve pounder guns sent aft, pointed out of his own stern windows. Normally, the ship carried no stern chasers, since the guns were more important on the broadside. In this case, with a heavy ship they could not safely face coming up in their wake, these guns were the only weapons he could strike with. The gunner and his crew worked feverishly to rig the new breeching tackle.

While the crews were getting all ready, Mister Daniels, their Marine lieutenant, approached and volunteered to captain a gun. Knowing Daniels had a keen eye, he accepted and also ordered Thomas Lane aft to captain the other gun. Lane had captained Number Six gun on this voyage and Phillips knew him to be a careful man and as liable as the next man to make his shots count. He had done exemplary service with Miss Humphries and he wished to give the fellow added responsibility.

The Constitution was following in their wake, slowly gaining. She had not fired recently. To do so would

130

require her to veer away to one side or another, in able to fire the foremost guns. This, of course, would cause the pursuer to fall back every time she swerved. Evidently her captain was content to bide his time and come up alongside where there could be no question of victory.

As the gunner pronounced the first gun secured, the gun crew began their drill. The flintlock had already been mounted on the breech, and the tompion had been removed earlier. A charge was inserted into the barrel and rammed home. A wad followed and the ball was rolled in. Another wad was rammed down on the ball to keep it from rolling out, then Mister Daniels took a gunner's pick and probed down through the vent and punctured the cartridge. A quill charged with priming powder was thrust down the vent into the charge and Daniels ordered the gun run out.

Glancing to see that everyone was clear of the gun and carriage, he grasped the lanyard and sighted down the barrel at the enemy, making certain he stood behind a chalk mark the gunner had made on the deck. The weight of the two guns had depressed the stern a bit, and the quoin appeared to be inserted improperly. With the muzzle pointing low, it should be raised a bit by pulling out the quoin. Not wanting to delay the shot until the matter was corrected, he merely waited until the stern lifted on a wave and then pulled the lanyard. With the roar of the gun and the violent recoil to the rear, Daniels faced the merest instant of terror as the monstrous mass of iron and oak slammed back to within few inches from his body before it was stopped by the breeching cables.

A cheer roared forth from the mouths of a hundred men as the ball was seen to impact her hull near her cutwater. This was a sensitive place on a ship, since a sprung plank could be the very devil to repair at sea. No sooner than the roar died down when the second gun fired. This also impacted the American's forward hull, and Phillips wondered how much longer the big ship would withstand this abuse before she came about and fired off her broadside.

If her gun crews were well worked up, that could well end the fight in an instant.

Now the wind was being fickle. Earlier, it had favored Constitution, but now it seemed to wish to humor Andromeda. She slowly began to draw away. A quick glance to Tenedos showed her hull down. That ship was not going to have an opportunity to influence the action.

Daniels fired again. With his quoin placed properly, the gun fired, high this time. Phillips would have advised against this shot, since it was aimed at the rigging, and it would be a very lucky shot to cause any damage with a single gun. Lucky it was though, since the shot clipped the topmast and put a substantial notch in it. Nothing fell away, but the spar was weakened. Constitution's captain, perhaps fearing the topmast might fail, sent topmen up to reduce sail to reduce the strain on the spar.

Lane fired his ball into the forward hull again, and now Constitution's yards began to swing around. The big ship was turning to port. Soon those twenty four pounder long guns would open on him. She also had a quantity of thirty two pounder carronades, but Phillips did not fear them overmuch at this stage of the game. He thought Constitution was just far enough away to limit the effect of those guns.

With Constitution turning to port, Phillips ordered Andromeda to do the same. He definitely did not want Constitution across his stern, firing all her guns right up Andromeda's arse. Constitution fired off a pair of her forward starboard twenty four pounders, putting a heavy ball into the wardroom, causing dreadful damage as it ranged forward. The first officer sent a party below to assist the carpenter in case he had any serious damage to contend with. Again and again the two ships exchanged blows, as they raced through the seas. The pair of guns at the stern became so hot, they were jumping from the deck, and Phillips ordered the charges reduced.

Their own ship was being gradually reduced to wreckage as the hull was being shot to pieces beneath them, especially the stern. The rudder mountings had been badly damaged and Phillips wondered how much longer they would have it. Fortunately, nothing important aloft had been hurt enough to slow them. Constitution, hampered by the crippling of her foremast, was slowly losing ground, and by nightfall it was apparent Andromeda was going to escape.

Tenedos had long since been left behind beneath the horizon, and with his crippled ship, Phillips had no desire to search for her.

A conference in the middle of night with his carpenter, the sailing master and first officer revealed the ship must make some important repairs before she could safely face the rigors of the open sea. The Constitution now far behind them in the dark, Andromeda turned toward land. It was necessary first to insure they were out of sight of Constitution by first light, then they must find a secure refuge to make repairs.

The masthead lookouts were sent up early, and all awaited the first reports. "Land ahead!" was announced, and there, well ahead, was a desolate looking shore. With no sign of any other shipping, Andromeda followed the shoreline. Mister Harding came up with a chart of these lands and indicated what he thought was their proximate position.

CHAPTER SEVENTEEN

They were apparently following a long, off-shore island. There was no hope of safety on this low-lying coast, but eventually, the island ended, and another began a mile ahead of them. Harding did not trust the chart, so the launch was put over the side and the boat crew took her ahead to check the depths. Proceeding slowly, with the depths sounded as they went, the ship moved along under her reefed tops'ls. Once through the channel between the two islands, they were in a passageway between the mainland and the next barrier island. Crawling along, with the ship's keel sometimes just feet above the bottom, they came to the mouth of a river.

The boat moved into the river and found just enough depth in a single channel to take the ship. The remaining boats were lowered and manned. With her sails furled, the boats pulled the ship into the river channel upstream as far as she would go. Phillips decided this was the best he could do. He felt the offshore island would protect them from any ordinary storm. This was hurricane country so that had to be considered, but he could do nothing about that problem for now.

Mister Daniels took a party of Marines to reconnoiter the terrain. Because of the marshy surroundings, the men were ordered to wear their normal ship-board attire, the same slop clothing the seamen wore. Their uniforms were left on the ship. The party of mud-smeared men returned late in the afternoon with their report. This area was low-lying and marshy, with hummocks of higher ground. Game seemed to be plentiful. No recent sign of men, although a fallen cabin and overgrown field was found upriver on some higher ground.

Chips reported to the captain that while he had much of the material needed for the more important repairs, he did need some heavy timbers to replace damage in the stern. The ship's sternpost must be built up, and the rudder repaired, as well as some framing issues taken care of.

There were many bigger trees available that could be harvested but the only available means of transportation was the river, so it would be necessary to find stands of the proper timber along the river's bank. Chips took a party armed with axes and saws to search. While they were gone, the crew began unloading the ship, especially the stern, to get it as far out of the water as was possible. A pair of boat guns were taken from the ship and emplaced ashore covering the likely approaches to the site.

That afternoon, the carpenter's crew came back accompanied by a strange looking man and a team of rough looking oxen dragging an oak log behind. The man was bearded and wore buckskin clothing, and a hat made of the hide of some small animal.

Phillips stepped back as the man approached and expectorated a stream of tobacco juice at his feet. The man held out a grimy hand and stated, "Jedediah Stuart here, gen'ral."

Phillips gingerly shook Stuart's free hand. The backwoodsman was holding a long rifle very similar to his own, save for the different ignition system.

Chips came forward. "Mister Stuart here met us as we were deciding whether to cut down this tree. He offered to haul it here with his team if we would pay him a Spanish dollar for it. I told him we would need another three just like it."

Phillips invited the woodsman onto the Andromeda and had his servant set up the deck chairs, and produce cups and a flagon of rum. Stuart downed the rum in one swallow and held out the cup for another.

"So, Mister Stuart, you can deliver three more logs like this one if we pay you four dollars?"

"Yessir Genr'al, I know that is highway robbery, but you'll get the logs a sight faster than if you try to drag 'em to the river and float 'em down. 'Sides, them logs are green an' won't float nohow!"

"Well Mister Stuart, you just sit right there and I will get your money." The cabin had been struck down and much of his furnishings taken ashore, but he knew just where his chest was located in the hold. Finding it, he withdrew his purse and found the dollars. Another long case beside the trunk held the long rifle he had purchased in Halifax. He took the rifle and hunting bag and went back up on deck.

In his absence, the woodsman had downed another mug of rum and his speech was becoming a little slurred. Phillips handed him the coins which were immediately secreted in his own hunting bag.

"Say, Gen'ral, where'd you get that rifle gun? My old pa had one like it. That was a Burkett, out of Lancaster.

137

"'Cept that lock on your'n was never made by Burkett. Looks like he didn't quite get it right, whoever did that."

"This rifle was made in Lancaster, Mister Stuart, although I don't know who made the weapon itself. A gunmaker in Halifax made the lock."

"Well, that 'splains it. Them Yankees never get anything right!"

"Oh, I don't know, Mister Stuart. This rifle shoots well for me."

"Well, I'd offer you a match, but your gun would never fire anyhow. I'll not take your money without a chance."

Phillips looked around. A small rill running into the river near the boat had washed a small branch onto a small sand bar. It was a stick, barely an inch in diameter and was probably a good ten fathoms away. Pointing at it, he asked Stuart if he could break the stick with a ball from his rifle.

"Well, sure I could, but you can't, and it wouldn't be right to shoot against you."

Phillips stood and retrieved a paper cartridge from his bag. Stuart eyed him curiously as he charged the weapon and extracted the cap from the brass box built into the buttstock. Placing the cap on the nipple, he asked Stuart if he would like to fire the rifle.

"Not me, Genr'l. I'll not have you laughing at me."

Phillips took a careful sight, then he eased the trigger back. The heavy long barrel hung steady on the target. The powerful mainspring slammed the hammer down on the cap which exploded instantly, firing the weapon. The stick jumped, broken into two pieces.

"I will be damned Mister! Just how in hell did that thing go off without a flint and frizzen?"

Phillips went over to an arms chest and removed a pistol from inside. He placed another cap on the iron strap reinforcing the cover and struck it with the pistol butt. A loud 'pop' sounded as the cap exploded. He showed Stuart how the flash from the cap communicated with the main charge inside the barrel.

"Well, this is all well and good, but just where would you go about getting these caps?"

"The only place I know of, Mister Stuart, is the gunmaker in Halifax, where I bought it."

"Well, there you go. When you run out of caps, or just lose 'em, you are out of luck. If I look around, I can find a hunk of flint in most any stream bed and make my own. Now, just when are you gonna be needing them other logs?"

"Just as soon as you can get to it, Mister Stuart. I see Chips is hewing out the first one you brought, already."

"Well, you see, I'm gonna have to let the team rest a bit. I don't have any grain to feed them. Just grazing, they don't last long before they tire."

"I have no grain, Mister Stuart. I could however give you a hundred pound bag of ship's biscuit. That might give them some energy to work."

The cattle wolfed down some biscuit and the hands followed Stuart back to the forest for the second log. By the time it had been felled and brought back to the ship, dusk was falling. Stuart left and promised to be back in the morning.

Chips and his crew labored on the project steadily for the next week. The sheathing in the stern had to be removed and some of the damaged frames repaired. Chips did not wish to take the time to completely replace the broken timbers, so he put them in their proper places and re-enforced them with timbers pinned over them with treenails. He was not satisfied with the green timber he needed to use, but made do with what he had. With fresh sheathing on the stern, he was ready to re-hang the rudder.

A week after they moored in the river, they were ready to begin caulking the repairs. With much of the important work done, it was now a matter of re-stowing the hold and getting everything aboard.

Stuart came back and offered to take Phillips hunting. With time now available, Phillips took Mister Daniels and his batman along and accompanied Stuart. After trudging through the swampy forest for hlours, Stuart left the pair behind a sumac thicket on a knoll. Ordering them to remain there, he told them he would send some meat their way. Phillips readied his rifle, while Daniels checked his personal fusil. This was a light weight weapon firing a heavy ball. Phillips had tried the weapon from the deck aboard ship and found it had a vicious recoil.

The pair soon heard Stuart coming though the undergrowth. Ahead of him a pair of whitetail deer stepped daintily to the edge of the clearing, then sensing danger, leaped forward. Caught by surprise, Phillips managed at the last minute to put the front sight of his rifle out in front of one of the deer and pull the trigger. That deer shot into the brush on the other side of the clearing and was gone.

He dimly remembered Daniel's fusil crashing but had not seen what happened. Stuart came out of the forest, going right to Daniel's deer, now folded up where it had fallen, at the edge of the clearing. The heavy ball had dropped it immediately. He went to the thicket and nodded to Phillips. "Here is your deer. She ran a ways after you hit her. These small rifle balls do not always stop them in their tracks. I like to hold on their neck, myself. Seems they go down faster."

A party from the ship arrived and dressed out the deer. Stuart was presented half of Phillips' deer. The remainder would feed him and the gunroom, while Daniels' meat would go to the wardroom.

The gig waited just off the beach while Phillips made his farewells. As he seated himself, Stuart wondered, "Say there Genr'al, I hear we're fighting the British agin. Know anything about that?"

Surprised, Phillips could only nod.

"Well, I guess we'll just have to whup 'em again just like my Pa did, years ago. You take care now, Genr'al, and watch out for them British!"

CHAPTER EIGHTEEN

Phillips boarded on the port side of the ship, without the usual ceremonial. He saw a party preparing to raise the ensign and called out. "Mister Wilson, I'd be glad for you to postpone that until we are out at sea. If anyone on this coast should see us, I'd prefer they did not know who we are."

With the damage that had been inflicted during the action with Constitution, Phillips felt he needed to have the ship surveyed in a good shipyard. It would be easier to sail up the coast to Halifax, but he knew the shipyard there was busy, and thought there might be an inordinate delay. Chips informed him the green wood they had used for repairs was sure to rot, and the sooner it could be replaced, the better.

Deciding the yard at English Harbor might be a better choice, they went south. The repairs done back on the mainland had been done in a hurry, and there was difficulty with leakage. There was no imminent danger to the ship, but it would be best if the ship not face any heavy weather before more complete repairs could be made.

It was a long trip, but they sailed into Antigua's English Harbor, and picked up their mooring after saluting the Admiral's flag. HMS Tenedos was floating proudly at her mooring, and many of her crew stopped what they were doing when they went by. He was pulled over to the flag expecting to see the admiral, but was told the man was indisposed with dropsy. The flag captain took care of his reports and said the dockyard would be notified of the necessary repairs.

"Now then", the flag captain began. "I understand you were in an action with the USS Constitution and supposedly taken or destroyed. Would you give me the news of what happened to you?"

Phillips had brought along his reports and log which the flag captain glanced through. "You say you obeyed a flag signal from Tenedos to engage the enemy. Could there have been a mistake in reading the signal?"

Phillips answered. "Sir, there were actually three such signals. One was 'Enemy in Sight', another "To engage the Enemy' and the final was 'Engage the Enemy More Closely'. We did as we were ordered, but Tenedos was unable to come up to assist and we were much beaten about."

Captain Ellis looked puzzled. "Phillips, you do know Captain Danson of Tenedos died of apoplexy two weeks before that action, do you not?"

Phillips was concerned. Danson was an old friend of the family who had often stayed at the Phillips estate back in his youth. "I did not, Captain Ellis. Who was commanding Tenedos at the time?"

"That would have been Lieutenant Granger, her first lieutenant."

Now Phillips was really puzzled. Granger had no business ordering a ranking officer as to when or how he was to engage the enemy.

Ellis broke the silence. "Captain, I want you to report back here this afternoon with your signal officer and his log. You should also bring along your first lieutenant and your master with his log."

Upon returning as ordered, the wan looking admiral was present but said nothing. Captain Ellis was certainly in charge. A few minutes after the party from Andromeda arrived, that from Tenedos entered. Ellis asked Phillips if he had ever met Lieutenant Granger. Phillips assured him that he had never met the man.

After the stilted introductions, Ellis began the proceedings. "Gentlemen, this is by no means an official inquiry, although a report will be submitted to Vice Admiral Sir Alexander Cochrane, Commander of the North America Station. Our purpose is to determine exactly who was responsible for the engagement between HMS Andromeda and the USS Constitution. If everyone will place their logs on the table, I would be obliged."

Ellis continued, "Beginning with Lieutenant Granger. Sir, will you tell me what duty you were performing on the day of the action?"

Granger looked pale and not at all well. "Sir, I was in command of HMS Tenedos, after the death of Captain Danson."

"Very well, Lieutenant. Will you tell us of the events of that day, starting of course before the action took place?"

"Yes sir, shortly after the lookouts were sent up, I heard the call from the maintop, 'Sail in sight off the port bow'. I went up on deck and sent an officer to the maintop with a glass. He reported the sighting to be a large ship. Hull down, her identity could not be determined at that time."

"Very good Mister Granger. Exactly when was her identity determined?"

"Probably a glass later, sir. My sailing master recognized her, having served in the Med when she was there."

"Fine, now, just who was she?"

"Why, the USS Constitution, sir."

"And what plans did you make immediately, Mister Granger?"

"Sir, I thought I had better stay out of her way. She is better armed and more strongly built than Tenedos. I felt I would not have a chance if I engaged her."

"What about if you had assistance. What if another King's ship were present to assist?"

"Then sir, I think there would have been a real chance to defeat her."

"Good. Now when did you become aware of the presence of Andromeda?"

"About a glass later. Again, our maintop lookout saw her west of Constitution."

"And what were your thoughts when you learned of her presence?"

Granger was looking paler by the minute. "Sir, we were unable to read her number at first, but thought she was a King's ship by the cut of her sails. She appeared to be a large ship-sloop or maybe a small frigate. Without knowing who she actually was, I thought she probably had either a commander or post captain commanding. I knew whoever it was would be superior in rank to myself and therefore in command of any joint action. When we could read her number I learned she was Andromeda, a post ship, and that Captain Phillips was in command."

"Now, at what time did you signal Captain Phillips that you commanded Tenedos?"

"Well, sir, I never actually told him that I was in command. I thought he already knew."

"Mister Granger, I myself did not know you were in command until afterward. HMS Andromeda was on detached duty. How was he supposed to learn of the death of Captain Danson?"

Granger stood mute and he was visibly trembling.

Captain Ellis continued, "Mister Granger. What signals were passed between Tenedos and Andromeda before the action?"

"No actual signals sir. We both made our numbers to each other."

"So you never signaled Andromeda to attack Constitution?"

"Oh no sir. I could not do that. Captain Phillips was senior to me."

Captain Ellis went to the table and picked up a log book. "This appears to be Tenedos signal log. I see no entry for any signals at the time in question. I wonder why that is? Surely, a simple greeting might be exchanged."

Granger made no reply.

"Now here we have the signal log from HMS "Andromeda. This shows several entries. The first two seem to be attempts to answer unreadable signals from Tenedos. The next shows the acknowledgement to a signal from Tenedos to Andromeda to 'Enemy in Sight'. Then we have another acknowledgement of a signal purportedly from Tenedos, 'Engage the Enemy'. Finally another acknowledgement from the same source, 'Engage the Enemy More Closely'. I wonder why the discrepancies?

Ellis eyed the log books closely then opened a drawer on his desk and withdrew a magnifying glass. "I have a little trouble reading fine writing, so am required at times to use this glass."

Peering closely through the glass, he exclaimed. "Gentlemen, I think I see the difficulty. A page has been cut from this log. I can just see the remains of the original page. Would you gentlemen care to examine this?"

Everyone but Granger took the opportunity to look at the log book. While he was looking at the page with his young eyes, Phillips thought he saw the traces of a sharp blade on the underlying page. He showed that to Captain Ellis, who could not make it out himself, but the admiral's flag lieutenant could see it quite clearly.

Captain Ellis reported. "Gentlemen, I see no need to continue this discussion. I intend to recommend to the admiral this matter be brought to the attention of Vice-Admiral Sir Alexander Cochrane for possible action. You are dismissed. Mister Granger, would you remain behind?"

CHAPTER NINETEEN

Back aboard the Andromeda, matters were now advanced. Her crew were busy again loading stores into the ship's boats to be delivered ashore. A preliminary survey had already been done, with some shaking of heads when rot was discovered in some of the older timbers. Phillips was awaiting a visit from the dockyard superintendent when a well-appointed launch came alongside, with a tall officer wearing a hussar uniform sitting in the sternsheets.

This man, piped aboard with all due ceremony, carried a summons to appear before the governor. The officer insisted the appointment could not wait, and offered to take him in his own boat. Mister Harding was observing the proceedings on deck and the third officer, Mister Wilson, was on duty. Calling these gentlemen over, he asked them to inform Mister Hornady he had been called away to meet with Governor Eliot.

Phillips had met Governor Eliot before and his servant ushered him right in. Unusually, Eliot did not begin the conversation with small talk, as he normally did. He got right to the point.

"Captain Phillips, this is in regard to your recent mission where you delivered a British envoy to meet with Señor Bolivar. Lord Forsythe has been obliged to flee along with Bolivar and has sailed on a local boat to an island just east of Spanish Puerto Rico. The Isla de Vieques by name. He has taken refuge with a fisherman's family on the island and asks that he be removed as soon as possible."

"He requests the Spanish authorities not be notified of his situation. It seems they believe he is somehow involved with the revolution on the mainland, and he is concerned about arrest and possible imprisonment. Lord Forsythe has been on this island a month already and there is concern of his health. I wish you to take your ship and proceed immediately to the island to retrieve him."

Phillips was disturbed. By now, he regarded Lord Forsythe as a friend, and would go to extremes to remove him from any danger. The problem was his ship. With the additional damage discovered by the dockyard people, there was real danger the ship might not return should she encounter any heavy weather. He indicated as much to the governor then informed him of the stores that had already been landed.

"Sir, would there be another vessel available that could make the trip?"

Eliot shook his head. "Not one that is not in worse condition than your own."

He thought a few minutes, then said, "Of course, there is Marseilles!"

"Marseilles, Governor?"

"Yes, she is a former French corvette you people brought in when you chased the French out of the Caribbean. She is a fairly new ship that has been let go to rack and ruin, and had to be towed back here behind HMS Arethusa. Our dockyard people have made a sort of pet of her and I am told she is now as good as new. However, she was unarmed when we took her from her mooring in Guadeloupe. She is complete but has neither guns nor crew."

"Sir, Andromeda has all of her guns and a fine crew."

"Yes Captain Phillips, she does indeed. Would you be prepared to take command of the corvette and sail her to the island of Vieques?"

"Yes sir, I would. Do we know the exact location where we may find Lord Forsythe?"

"Yes Captain, we do. We do have a hand-drawn sketch which will be in your hands in a moment. I will call my naval aide in to explain all of the details of the ship to you. I do have a busy morning so you would oblige me if you met with Lieutenant Raines just down the hall. My servant will take you."

The governor added, "Just one more matter, Captain. The Marseilles was not the only French warship left behind. One of their forty gun frigates had been laid up in a creek mouth before our troops came in and took the island. She had been more or less abandoned for lack of stores and her men had gone onto various privateers. Before retreating the French made a try at firing her, but it had rained all of the previous night and the fire did not take hold."

"Our troops had other things on their minds than a dilapidated, abandoned French ship, so they mentioned it in a dispatch and went on to other things. The war passed that region by and the ship was forgotten. Some pirates, some of them perhaps former crewmen, found her and was able to move her to another mooring."

"We hear now those pirates have got her back at sea and are using her to take respectable sized commercial vessels. We have no idea as to how she is now armed or the number of her crew. Normally, we would hesitate to ask an officer to bring a forty gun frigate to action with a much lighter post ship, but the expectation is she does not have all of her guns, and it is doubtful if she has a professional commander."

"Should you encounter her, perhaps you could see what we have to deal with. Understand your first business must be to recover Lord Forsythe."

With that, Governor Eliot shook his bell and a servant led Phillips off. As he went out the door, Eliot pressed a scrap of paper in his hand. A crude map of Lord Forsythe's location on a tiny island was scratched on it.

A one armed naval officer was waiting in the anteroom and introduced himself. Phillips asked him about the ship.

"Well, the French used her as a twenty gun corvette, what we might use as a sloop of war. She was probably armed with French eight pounder guns, but the shipwright over at the dockyard tells us she could carry our twelve pounders. He also thinks we could put a pair of twenty four pounder carronades on the quarterdeck, with maybe a pair of twelve pounder carronades up forward. We do have a few carronades in the dockyard but no long guns available."

Phillips nodded, "Andromeda will be going into the dockyard for a complete re-build and will be landing all of her guns. We can use her long twelves to arm the Marseilles."

Raines said, "We are going to have to do something about that name. The admiral is still under the weather, so I will check with flags about a new one."

151

Raines continued, "That was a terrible shame about Granger, wasn't it, sir?"

"What about Granger?"

"Well, after the hearing, he couldn't be found. A note found in the ante-room announced he had resigned his commission. He left the building without notice and later was seen boarding a local schooner that does a little trading about the Caribbean. He is listed on Tenedo's books as 'Run' and the search is on for him. Apparently, he falsified the ship's log books to corroborate his own story. Both the signal officer and midshipman confessed to the fraud, as did the master. All said they were forced to do so."

With pressure from the governor, and unseen pressure from the sickbed of the admiral, matters moved quickly. Andromeda had been warped alongside a quay, and guns, stores and equipment were hoisted aloft, swung out over the side and lowered onto ox-drawn wains. The carts were then hauled over to the quay where Marseilles was tied and the process reversed.

The governor furnished some funds to hire extra labor and Phillips dug into his purse and supplied more. As a man completed his task on Andromeda, he was sent to the new ship to start there. In the midst of this confusion, Governor Eliot came to the dockside in his carriage to inspect the proceedings. After some casual conversation, he handed over the ship's commission to Phillips. "She is to be the post ship HMS Roebuck, of the sixth rate."

With the commission, the governor took a canvas packet from his servant and handed it to Phillips. "This is your signal book. You will, of course, preserve it from capture by the enemy."

The packet as Phillips took it was heavy, and he knew there were weights inside that would sink it if thrown overboard.

Most of the old crew of Andromeda had transferred over to Roebuck, with the exception of the standing officers. These included the sailing master, cook, bosun, gunner, carpenter and clerk. Phillips regretted having to leave these men behind. They would stay with Andromeda, and after she was whole again would sail under the command of a different captain.

Once aboard Roebuck, it was necessary for everyone to find his place and acquaint himself with the new people. Phillips had barely stepped into his barren office when Mister Hornady knocked and reported, "Sir, I have all the new warrants outside, whenever you want to see them."

"Very well. Let us do that on the quarterdeck. I have not so much as a stool here. We'll go up top and stand."

It was obvious that some of the new warrants had been selected hastily, some, perhaps before their time. The acting sailing master who reported to him first was a very young former master's mate. Mister Layton had had a dozen years at sea, as midshipman and master's mate, and now seemed to be going up the ladder another rung. Phillips was assured by the new warrant he had the required charts of the areas in which they would likely be sailing. Concerned he might lose the scrap of paper with the location of Lord Forsythe, he handed it to Layton and asked him to copy it and add it to the relevant chart.

"We will be sailing to that location Mister Layton, and will there take on board a very important passenger, so this paper is a most essential document."

After dismissing the Master, he saw a massively built individual was shifting on his feet, obviously impatient to be about some task. With some effort, he recalled this was their new Gunner, previously gunner's mate from a third-rate that was, at this moment, now beating out of the harbor. Gunner's Mate Adams had been removed willy-nilly from his seventy-four line-of-battle ship against the fervent objections of his captain, and now found himself Gunner aboard Roebuck.

Phillips knew the warrant had much work to do to get all of the Andromeda's guns aboard besides locating the needed carronades hidden somewhere in the dockyard. Without ado, he shook the man's hand and sent him to his job.

The Carpenter was a very important man aboard ship, and this one was the only standing officer that had served previously in that capacity before. As carpenter on a thirty-eight gun frigate, Mister Sommers had contracted fever here on the island and had nearly died. When he recovered, his ship had sailed and he was without a job for the first time in two decades. Now all was right with the world, and he had a sound ship to keep in good repair.

Unlike Mister Sommers, the new cook had absolutely no experience whatsoever. Mister Hatter had been a former topman who had had a leg shot off in an action a year before. Recently released from hospital, he had been offered the position of cook aboard Roebuck. As such, he was not required to have any familiarity with the task. This was mainly a lifetime sinecure which would keep him employed for the rest of his life.

His main tasks would be to see the provisions supplied for the crew's meals were as edible as possible. He would keep the numbered metal disks which would be fastened to each of the messes boiling bags in which the salt beef or pork was cooked. The person from each mess that had been designated mess-cook would clip the disk to a bag with the proper amount of salt meat and watch over it as it cooked. When done, the bag would be retrieved from the big copper, the disk removed and given back to the cook and the meat taken back to the mess where it would be divided and served.

The Bosun was also a young man. He would be responsible for the ships' lines and cables, boats and anchors. He also oversaw punishment of those crewmembers convicted at Captain's Mast of various crimes. Bosun Bailes was also a most important member of the crew. Any laxity on his part could well lead to the loss of the ship.

After interviewing the new standing officers, Phillips looked over the side and saw a welcome sight coming down the stone quay. A heavy wagon was groaning and clattering its way along the cobblestone pavement with its load of captain's furnishings and stores from Andromeda. His desk, table and bed were there along with a few chairs and his own personal stores for the next voyage.

Nero, his servant, was instructing the hands where to stow the various articles. The former slave had been savagely whipped, at one time in his life, which had almost destroyed his body. With little strength these days, he usually acted as a supervisor, instructing others what they needed to be doing. He was a most useful crewmember, the only fault being his unusual accent. He had been born a slave on a British island, where many of the slaves on the sugar plantations were fresh from Africa and spoke a bewildering number of languages. The slaves developed their own patois, which varied from island to island. Then, as an adult, he was bought by a Dutch owner and taken to another island where he had to learn a new Dutch-based patois.

Now, he was a freeman on a Royal Navy ship, at least as free as any seaman could be, black or white. Nero took the opportunity to hand him a note, actually penned by a midshipman, listing supplies that must be purchased. Nero was terrified to go ashore here in the Caribbean by himself. A slave was a rather valuable piece of property here, and it would be only too easy for some unscrupulous sort to snatch a black from the street and sell him to some planter. Whenever Phillips sent Nero ashore to obtain something, he always tried to send at least a midshipman with him, usually accompanied by a pair of powerful hands who would see that he did not end up in the wrong place.

CHAPTER TWENTY

At length, the Royal Marines marched up to the quay and came aboard. Lieutenant Hasting commanded the two dozens of Marines with the help of a sergeant and a corporal. The ship was filling up now, with hardly space to "Swing a Cat" as the Bosun often stated. The cat he referred to was the 'cat-o'-nine tails', a lash used to punish wayward crewmen.

With her water, guns and stores aboard, Roebuck moved out into the harbor where she took aboard her powder. During this exercise, all fire of any sort was extinguished and men went barefoot, as they passed the little kegs of explosive aboard. The gunner and his mates stowed the powder in the magazine. Most of the powder was of the high quality furnished by the Navy, but some of it had been privately purchased by Captain Phillips.

This would necessarily be used for target practice, since Admiralty did not allow for what they termed excessive firing at targets. One could use as much of the King's powder as one wished in firing at enemy ships and installations, but not at targets.

Phillips' target powder was formerly French issue, captured, and now perhaps to be used against them.

As powder was carefully brought aboard, water was continually swabbed on the deck to drench any tiny spills that might occur. No ferrous metals, iron or steel, was allowed near the barrels of powder. Even the bands holding the barrel staves together were of copper. It was absolutely necessary there should be no opportunity for a spark to explode the powder.

Now, with everything needed aboard, Roebuck sailed. This should be an easy and fast voyage. They merely had to sail downwind past a string of islands, St. Kitts, St. Croix and the approaches to the Spanish island of Puerto Rico.

Islas de Vieques, a small island near the eastern end of Puerto Rico itself, was their destination. Mister Layton, the acting master remained on deck as they neared Vieques. Before leaving Antigua, he had sought as much instruction as was available on the island and had interviewed several seamen and fishermen who had recently visited the place. Making the required corrections on his charts as needed, he was prepared to give his captain needed advice.

Upon reaching their destination, Phillips turned to Layton and asked him to take over the ship. Standing back, he watched Layton conn the ship past a rocky point protruding out into the sea and then closing a thick mangrove forest along the shore. At this point, Phillips was ready to take back the ship, since there seemed to be no protective bay in which to anchor the ship. He was not about to anchor off a lee shore for any length of time.

Turning to Phillips, Layton said, "The chart shows there should be a bay behind these mangrove trees. I would like to anchor and send a boat in to look." They dropped the hook and Layton went over the side into the launch with a boat crew. As the boat approached a solid wall of green vegetation, the bowman was seen to reach out with a boathook and divide the greenery. The oarsmen pulled the boat right inside and it was gone.

Phillips was getting nervous with the wait, and ordered a swivel gun loaded to fire off a demand the boat return forthwith. Just as the gunner was reaching into the binnacle to get a light for his slowmatch, the vegetation parted and the boat appeared.

Reporting aboard, Layton announced the bay was inside and deep and large enough to take the ship. The entrance was just barely navigable, but they would need to clear some of the mangrove roots and trunks before towing the ship inside. He recommended they send a pair of boats with saws and axes to clear away a path before trying to fit the ship through.

Expecting this could be a lengthy task, Phillips did not want to leave the ship in this exposed position on the lee shore, so they pulled up anchor and, after leaving a pair of boats and their crews behind, sailed out to sea. They would return at dusk to take the men aboard, to be out of reach of the expected mosquitos.

Mister Layton wished to remain behind, but Phillips reasoned that the boat crews could function without him, and he wished to know what Layton could tell him.

He learned there was no colonization of the island by the Spanish. The chief residents were outlaws and pirates, with a few scattered fishing families. Layton had learned that Spanish authorities on Puerto Rico had become tired of the depredations of these pirates and there was talk of mounting an offensive against them. He himself thought the pirates had also learned of this and had already moved their base of operations elsewhere. It might be wise though, to recover Lord Forsythe as quickly as possible and depart before becoming discovered by the Spanish.

There were no signs of man in the enclosed lagoon. A note scratched on the crude map he had received mentioned firing off a gun at unstated intervals. Phillips hesitated firing off one of the great guns, fearing it would be recognized by what it indeed was and attract undue attention. Instead, he had the gunner prepare a swivel gun and lay some of the miniature charges near it.

One of the landsmen, with no particular shipboard skills, was tasked to stand by the gun and fire it every glass. Landsman Evers held up his linstock, with its smoldering slow-match, like a badge of office. Mister Hornady spoke to the fellow and required he put the linstock down, with the match over a tub of water. There was more than a little danger here with a burning match and live charges for the gun.

Every half hour, as the glass by the binnacle was turned, the gun banged, fired with its reduced charge. For much of the day there was no sign of a reply, but toward dusk, a figure was seen at water's edge, peering through the brush at the strange ship. The stranger stepped into a dug-out canoe hidden nearby and paddled out to Roebuck.

The fellow was roughly clad in what appeared to be mostly rags and carried a large cane knife that showed a gleaming edge where it had recently been sharpened. The black climbed the line tossed to him and stood before Phillips gazing around this strange ship, probably the largest edifice he had ever been in or on.

Phillips spoke to him, but the man spoke no English. French was tried, which also did not work. Finally Seaman Rodriguez was brought aft and asked to try. Rodriguez was a Spaniard who had found reason to sign on a British warship early on in the first war and showed no desire to return to his native land. His Spanish got at least a limited response from the stranger. Phillips instructed Rodriguez what he wished to learn from the fellow, and he tried.

Rodrigues, after speaking to the man and listening carefully, told his captain. "Sir, this man speaks a dialect I have never heard of before. He does know a few Spanish words, but pronounces them differently than I have ever heard. I think he wants to leave now. Maybe he will bring someone here, but when, I do not understand."

Phillips had some hands gather up some small tools the stranger might possibly find some use for and waved goodbye. In moments, the dugout was ashore, and he was gone.

No more was seen or heard of him that evening. It was felt there was no further need of the signal gun, so the charges were taken back to the magazine and Landsman Evers sent back to his normal duties.

It was late in the afternoon watch the next day when people were seen loading in the dugout. The stranger from yesterday, a frail looking black woman and a feverish white man.

The white man, apparently unable to sit, was laid in the canoe and the blacks took their places at bow and stern and paddled out to Roebuck. A boat crew scrambled down to the launch which was pulled up alongside and helped unload the canoe's passenger into the boat. Utterly helpless, he was laid on a wide board and hoisted up on deck, where Doctor Baynes took him into his custody.

The black stranger from yesterday pulled himself up a line with agility and began a lengthy explanation in his own language.

Not understanding a word, Phillips gave orders that a package, prepared the evening before, be brought up and given to the man. It contained some ship's biscuit, fish hooks and line, several knives and an axe. A musket and twenty cartridges were also handed to the fellow. When the woman climbed up the side as nimbly as the man, Phillips pulled his purse from his pocket and handed her ten Spanish dollars. Both were smiling broadly as they went down into their boat.

The afternoon hour were waning, but Hornady thought they could get the ship out of the passageway before dark. So, with the anchor brought up, the boats began pulling Roebuck through the narrow channel. In the growing darkness, the ship once touched an underwater obstruction, from which the boats could not free her. Soundings around the ship indicated depth enough.

Layton and Bosun Bailes discussed the situation and it was felt the ship was in the grasp of some underwater mangrove roots or branches. There seemed to be a certain amount of movement when both boats pulled. Phillips was ready to order the kedge dropped ahead of the ship so they could use the capstan to pull her out, but Layton suggested getting a little sail on the ship to try that idea first.

There was concern about ripping off some copper from the ship's bottom, but the first and most important tasks were to get the envoy to safety and to get the ship out of Spanish waters before they were discovered. In the end, it was felt any minor underwater damage could be taken care of back in English harbor.

Headsails were set to the wind, and without much of a protest, the ship pulled herself free of whatever was holding her. Free of the land, Roebuck spread her sails and was off.

CHAPTER TWENTY ONE

Once out at sea, Phillips went below to see to his passenger. Doctor Baynes told him Lord Forsythe had suffered a bad case of fever, but surprisingly seemed to be recovering.

Baynes allowed him to visit the patient for a few minutes only. Forsythe was able to inform him of a few of his escapades after the revolution failed and his efforts to engage passage on a small fishing vessel, only to fall ill on the way back. He said he had paid to be taken to the nearest British port, but had instead had been dropped off at Vieques and left in the care of a poor fisherman and his wife.

Forsythe reported they had brought him back from certain death by the use of some strange bark they continued to make him consume. The envoy was certain he would be in trouble with the foreign Office since all of his papers and reports had disappeared on the fishing vessel that had abandoned him.

The weakened man had news of the pirate frigate he had been warned about back in English Harbor. He did not know its present location but his caregivers had warned him of its presence on the island and warned him to stay well away from it.

"Were you able to understand his lingo, Milord?"

"We did manage to get along in his tongue. I already was familiar with Spanish, and we learned to communicate together in his patois. I heard him attempting to warn you of the pirate frigate but you did not understand."

"Could you tell me what you know about the ship, Lord Forsythe?"

"First let me tell you that Pedro, the only name the fellow had, is one of the finer people I know. He put his very life at terrible risk to help me, a perfect stranger. He is an intelligent person, wise in the ways of his environment. But, he does not know anything of our ways and has a limited vocabulary,"

"He was able to describe the ship and the men. He described them as 'devils', which may tell us something. He knew the term for 'guns' and said the ship had many. It is my thinking that we may not wish to encounter this ship unless we have to."

Forsythe had no first hand intelligence of the pirate and they left him to his rest. Before leaving his side, Phillips assured him he would make the strongest efforts to inform his superiors of the extraordinary exertions Forsythe had put forward to succeed in the mission. The envoy assured Phillips he could not really care. His main mission now was to return home to his wife and son. He had no intention of leaving the home shores again.

Phillips regarded his duty to get Lord Forsythe back north to a healthier climate, so was reluctant to sail back to Antigua. Far out to sea now, he spotted a small convoy bound for the islands, and was able to drop off a letter aboard one of the escorts advising Governor Eliot of the completion of the mission.

Captain Randolph, of the eighteen gun ship sloop Venus, reported seeing a forty gun French frigate yesterday. Her consort, a sixteen gunned brig, came up like a champion, and the two acting in concert seemed to have convinced the frigate to go elsewhere.

"It was my understanding", said Randolph, "that all of the French forces and ships had been accounted for in these parts."

Phillips related what he knew of the matter and asked he relay the intelligence to others. Randolph did say that when the frigate ran out her guns, all the ports did not open. He said he thought she might not be fully armed.

It was plain sailing up the eastern seaboard of America. At this stage of the war, a firm blockade was in place and there was little chance to encounter an enemy warship, although he had been warned there were still a few fast schooners about. Some of these would fill their holds with such produce as was plentiful in that area, obtain a few guns and a letter of marque, and attempt to sail to a port where they could sell their cargo at a fat profit. Should they encounter a British merchant ship, that of course was all to the good.

Actually, Phillips had learned, that did not usually work out well. Even if the schooner could evade the blockading ship, chances were their prizes could not, so the British ships often ended back up in friendly hands.

The Roebuck lookouts spotted sails of a few schooners who Phillips thought were probably enemy privateers, but he had no intention of pursuing them. Although Roebuck was a fast ship, she could not compete with one of the Yankee built schooners. Sailing up the seaboard, he sometimes wished he had the old Andromeda back, with her drab sides and the appearance of a fat trader. Roebuck looked like what she was, or had been, a French-built corvette. He doubted any Yankee privateer could be fooled by any disguise he could apply to her.

He had been told, however, some of these former corvettes had been purchased at prize auctions by commercial interests who intended to load the hulls with high value cargo and sail without fear of being taken by privateers.

Following the shipping lanes up the Gulf Stream, Roebuck was off the coast of Virginia, when a sleek schooner came out of the morning haze and approached them. Phillips had no interest in the vessel at all. He well knew it could outrun him, and he had Lord Forsythe aboard, whose safety he considered to be of overriding importance.

The schooner began making threatening runs on Roebuck, always sheering off before coming into long gunshot range. Again and again this happened. Phillips refused to be lured into attempting to attack or evade. Roebuck just continued on-course under easy sail. Her gun ports closed, she looked to perhaps really be an in-offensive former warship now put to civilian tasks.

Phillips had the thought in his mind this privateer could not actually endanger his ship, and while he could not catch her, neither could she do harm to him. He intended to continue on course and let the schooner act the fool if she so wished.

Just to keep everybody honest, he had ordered Mister Hornady to have the ship prepared for action, but the gunports should remain closed, and the match in the linstocks should not be lit. The smoke from such could be an indicator to an enemy that she might be armed and dangerous.

Finally, on one of the schooners rushes, she did not veer away before coming into gun range. Phillips did not respond. He had Lord Forsythe's safety to consider, and saw no reason to endanger it. He let his mind drift, wondering how he should respond to Forsythe's repeated invitations to visit his home and meet his wife and child again.

He was suddenly surprised when the schooner appeared close in, then turned on her heel and raced to the rear.

Mister Hornady came up. "Sir, I think that fellow may be getting his nerve up to attack us."

"I do believe you are right, Mister Hornady. How are the guns loaded?"

"Ball in the twelve pounder long guns, grape in the twenty-four pounder carronades, and canister in the twelve pounder carronades."

"I see. That could really spoil his day. Let us see if he makes another rush like that last. If he does, I'll want to see if we can get some damaging hits with the long guns. If we do, I'll try to close him to see what we can do with the carronades. I want to be careful not to let him get too close. He's probably filled with boarders."

168

The schooner had come about astern of Roebuck and was making another approach. This time she appeared to be shaving matters a little close. She came up from astern just off to port with her guns run out. Mister Hornady sent his midshipmen messenger to the guns telling the gunners they would be firing this time.

As the sleek predator closed in on Roebuck's port quarter her forward starboard gun fired. It was only a four pounder, but at that close range, punched a hole through Roebucks port beam. Curses sounded as somebody was peppered with splinters. As previously arranged, Mister Layton had taken the ship so Captain Phillips would be free to fight her.

Seeing his opportunity, Layton had the ship turned to port a few points which brought some guns to bear. One of them was the forward twelve pounder carronade loaded with canister. Being such a short weapon, its crew could slew it around farther than one of the long guns. Of course, there was the danger of upset, also.

Dozens of men were standing by the schooner's starboard rail, waiting for their chance to board. The blast of small shot from that gun cut a bloody swath through that throng. As the ship came around further, more of the guns bore. The long guns delivered the twelve pound balls through the thinly constructed sides of the schooner, then the big carronades sent their loads of grapeshot into the privateer.

The private schooner spun around and tried to claw her way free, but then one of the long twelves, firing at close range put a ball into her foremast. Her starboard shrouds had mostly been parted from the grapeshot, and the load on the mast was too great. The mast at the impact site, already severely stressed at the impact site, began to crack. Finally the load on the mast caused it to snap under the pressure. The mast, with its canvas and rigging fell to port overboard, and the drag in the sea brought the schooner right around. As she turned, she was able to fire off a few of her guns. By now, most of the fired guns on Roebuck had been reloaded, and they slammed their loads of grape into the now wrecked schooner. Roebuck came across the privateer's bow and lay there with her guns trained down the length of her hull.

The schooner's master wisely took the opportunity to haul down his flag. Again, Phillips had to deal with a large number of prisoners. The schooner had a pair of launches towing behind, which were undamaged. An armed boarding party went aboard and began sorting out the people. Any obvious seamen and the officers were sent on board Roebuck. Most of the privateer's crew were dedicated boarders, men who were probably not trained followers of the sea.

Laborers, farmers, anyone needing money could sign onto one of these privateers. They would not be paid, but would get a share of any money from the sale of any captured ship and cargo. In this case, the men would get nothing and those wounded or killed would have suffered in vain.

Phillips loaded as many of the privateer's landsmen into the launches as possible. These men he felt would not much of a danger to British commerce. It was the trained seamen he wished to keep away from the sea and resuming their career in attacking that commerce. He put two seamen in each boat to help insure it reached shore, but the rest of the skilled men were left aboard either the schooner or put onto Roebuck.

After the boats set sail for the mainland, Roebuck and her prize set out on the voyage home, the schooner under tow. As they proceeded north, Chips and his crew worked aboard the prize, making necessary repairs. One of the last projects was the erection of a jury foremast. Roebuck had an extra spar which could be made to do the task.

Extra skilled hands were needed for the task. A dozen Americans below, when offered a promise they would not be forced to fight against their countrymen, voluntarily agreed to assist with erecting the spar. It was shorter than the former foremast, but would have to do. The butt of the broken original was trimmed off six feet above the deck, with the base of the spar abutted up against it. A heavy line running through a block on the summit of the main was rigged to the spar and to the windlass. One party of men on the windlass cranked the spar upright, while others manned preventer lines attached to the new mast to keep it from swinging.

As the mast rose, more men began lashing the base of the new mast to the butt of the old. Lines previously fastened to the top would serve as temporary stays, to keep it erect. With the mast erect, the stays and shrouds, made up in advance, were installed and tightened. Finally, the old fore topmast was rigged as a lateen yard and the sailmaker and his crew set to work fabricating a new sail.

When finished, the schooner was not the handsome craft it had been before its adventure, but it could keep up with Roebuck, which was all that Phillips required. The Americans who had helped rig the schooner faced some hostility from their countrymen, so they were transferred over to Roebuck with the promise they would be freed and set ashore in Halifax. Phillips assured the men he himself would not press any of them, but he could not guarantee other British captains in the port would honor that pledge themselves. He told them they would be well advised to seek work ashore there until they had opportunity to return to the States.

Roebuck entered harbor and fired off the salute to Vice-Admiral Herbert Sawyer. He was promptly ordered aboard the hulked two decker Sawyer was using as his temporary flag. Still in delicate health, Lord Forsythe had been judged able to be pulled over to the flag as long as he was well wrapped against the cold.

Aboard the flag, the flag lieutenant took the documents carried by Phillips and ushered the pair into the great cabin. Sawyer sat at his desk with his stocking feet propped upon a blanket-wrapped porcelain jug of hot water. Suffering from a cold, the admiral sniffed and sneezed while they were present.

Sawyer mentioned he was impressed by the seamanlike manner Phillips had pulled off the rescue and wondered how he liked the Roebuck. When Phillips praised the ship, the flag lieutenant mentioned he had used it to nab yet one more Yankee privateer on the way north. "A fine looking schooner", he reported. "Re-armed, it would make a fine command for some officer."

"Meaning yourself, you mean," the admiral quipped. "As long as I have to suffer here, so do you, Anderson."

While Phillips and the admiral were discussing the past mission, Anderson was sorting through the documents Phillips had delivered. Just as Phillips was wondering if he should volunteer to leave or wait 'till he was told, Anderson gave a little start and interrupted the admiral in mid-sentence, shoving a sheaf of papers in front of him.

From the disgusted conversation between the two, Phillips soon grasped the subject was the missing first officer of Tenedos back in English Harbor. In Phillips hearing, the admiral ordered Granger's arrest when found. When found, he was to be brought back in chains.

After a few more minutes of discussion, Sawyer dismissed Phillips. He was told to expect orders within days, and was told to take aboard what supplies he needed.

CHAPTER TWENTY TWO

The work went rapidly and Roebuck was just waiting for orders to sail. He was on the quarterdeck watching a shore boat make its way out in the harbor, expecting it might be delivering an order for cabin stores he had sent for. There were too many people in the boat however. Three of them were Americans he had landed here after they assisted in some ship work on the way north. He had promised to set them ashore and he had. Now, they were climbing the side of the ship and explaining themselves to the anchor watch.

The master's mate led the trio aft and reported the men wished to speak with him. The spokesman explained the other Americans at liberty ashore treated them as pariahs and threatened them with the punishments they would receive when they returned to the States.

Phillips was sympathetic but had no idea what he was to do about their problem. "Well, what do you want me to do for you? You will not serve against your countrymen, and I have no place for men who will not fight."

"We are seamen, Captain Phillips. Could you give us berths as topmen, where we wouldn't have to shoot at Americans?"

Phillips answered, "Never let it be said I turned down a good topmen. You understand though, sooner or later the ship will be paid off and you will be sent aboard another ship. The captain of that ship may very well not be sympathetic to your wishes of avoiding combat."

"Oh, that's all right, Captain. This part of the war won't last much longer anyway. Then the ship will pay off and we'll sign on to some merchant on her way to India or China."

Hornady took the men in hand to get their names in his book, while Phillips gazed out over the harbor at the boat approaching. It was coming direct toward Roebuck and it looked to be on official business. A natty looking lieutenant climbed aboard and presented his packet to Phillips, with the added message that Admiral Sawyer wished to see him at his earliest convenience,

Knowing full well that meant he was to be on the flagship instantly, Phillips dropped down into the officer's boat so that he wouldn't have to wait until his own had been prepared. As he went down the side, he told Hornady to have his own boat sent to the flag to bring him back when the admiral was finished with him.

Admiral Sawyer had a worried expression on his face when Phillips entered the great cabin. "You reported earlier of a French frigate turning pirate down south. I have received similar reports from other sources. Today I learned that frigate got into one of our convoys and raised hell. Took off with two fat merchantmen. The Exchange in London will have my guts. I have nobody else available to go after the pirate, so I am sending you. Have you any thoughts?"

175

"We can be on the way as soon as the winds serve to get us out of harbor, sir."

Admiral Sawyer mused, "I know putting a twenty-four gun post ship up against a forty gun frigate is daft, but maybe not as bad as it may seem. We suspect she may not have all of her guns, and what is she doing for men? She won't have professional officers aboard, and her crew is probably just scum, with no discipline. I think you will be alright."

Going back to Roebuck, Phillips knew it was very well for the admiral to think things would be alright, but it would be up to himself and his crew to make them that way. On the weeks long voyage, Phillips exercised his guns every day, until he had expended all of his privately purchased ammunition. They took a week long hiatus then, but coming across an island off the coast of Georgia, Phillips pointed to a pile of rocks at the water's edge.

"Mister Hornady, I believe there could be some guns behind those rocks."

"Oh sir, surely not. Those are just rocks."

"Mister Hornady, I am your captain. That means I am wiser than you. I think there are enemy guns there and I intend to fire on them. Would you ready the starboard side guns, please?"

The ship ran past the island at two cables length distance firing each gun deliberately. Of course, every man on the ship knew very well there were no guns ashore, but they also knew the captain wanted to get in some more practice. Afterward, the log was duly brought up to date with the entry, 'two guns sighted on Jackson Island. Fired starboard broadside, destroyed battery'.

The men did not really need the practice now, since they had previously been well schooled, but every few days, Phillips would attempt to find a reason to fire a few shots.

At length, Roebuck came to the vicinity of the Bahamas. He did not approach any of the islands, remaining out to sea, but a pair of local armed brigs came out to inspect him. He received more word of the pirate frigate. It seemed she was becoming stronger. She was taking guns and ammunition from her prizes, and word was, she was gaining plenty of recruits.

This war had trained plenty of privateer's men. Laws of the sea were strict with what such people could do or could not do. Some thought it more profitable to turn pirate so they need not be squeamish about whether a potential target was legal quarry or not.

Roebuck sailed farther south, down past Spanish Cuba and Puerto Rico. Phillips heard some sad tales of the excesses of the pirate but no sign of her was seen. Stores were running low, so they put into English Harbor to obtain their wants. Governor Eliot again met with Roebuck's officers, giving them what little accurate information that he had.

There was one benefit of this port call. The salt beef they had taken aboard here had a different flavor that the old beef they had been using. Too, the purser took on casks of fresher lemon and lime juice to mix with their grog. A few cases of incipient scurvy cleared right up and Doctor Baynes, who had been constantly preaching to anyone that would listen to him that the old juice they had used before was suspect, was now pronounced a wizard for curing the scurvy.

A quantity of old, captured French powder was available for purchase, and Phillips bought all that he could stow in the magazine. It was old and of poor quality because of improper storage, but Gunner Adams assured him with enough time, he could dry it out until it was as good as any made in England. Some of the crew groaned to themselves, since this would mean plenty of gun practice, and the labor of heaving the heavy guns and carriages to battery.

After leaving English Harbor Roebuck continued south, stopping at every major island and many of the smaller island groups. Many time, they learned they had missed the pirate by just a few weeks. Phillips thought about finding the port where the pirate was taking his spoils, but decided they were mostly stripping their captures of anything they could sell, then delivering that to ports in the nearby Spanish Empire.

Spain, still involved in a terrible war back home, was also troubled with wars of independence here in the Americas, and was unable to police its own territories. The officers spent many a night in the great cabin agonizing over the question of where the big frigate could be based without being too obvious. Certainly, hundreds of ships were looking for the pirate but its location was a complete mystery.

Ranging down to Brazil, nothing was found. At least, they learned there was no sign of the frigate this far south. Some of the officers took part in a hunt on an island off the mainland. With his rifle, Phillips knocked down a young pig at well over a hundred yards, while Lieutenant Hastings, their Marine officer, bagged a wild goat.

It was not possible to hang the game long in view of the sweltering heat, so it was decided the captain and wardroom officers would dine on fresh pig tonight, while the goat would be tendered to the midshipmen for their own feast in the gunroom.

Since the captain was furnishing the meat, the other officers offered the wardroom for the meal. Much of the officers wine supply was now exhausted, so Phillips had his servant rummage around in his store and ferret out a five gallon little cask of a rather fiery liquor he had purchased at Cape Colony in South Africa long ago. There was actually nothing special about the spirits but it was different from the ubiquitous rum and therefore popular that evening. The officers had a riotously good time that evening and suffered accordingly the next morning.

On his solitary pacing on the quarterdeck, Phillips was attempting to walk off a monumental hangover. One fragmental memory of the evening before kept running through his brain. He very dimly recalled having an intense discussion with Doctor Baynes, in which they solved all of the world's problems.

CHAPTER TWENTY THREE

Phillips knew well these were but the maundering thoughts of a pair of drunks, but somehow, at the time, they thought they had discovered the location of their quarry. Dismissing these useless thoughts from his mind, he walked about the deck, examining everything he could think of. After finishing this, he pulled himself into the mizzen shrouds and began climbing. The crew in the immediate area looked upon him with some concern, since they well knew of his activities the evening before, and they also knew he was in no fit state to be climbing around in the tops.

Stubbornly, he kept climbing in the face of his men's disapproval until he reached the mizzen top. Here was a problem. There was a perfectly good opening next to the mast itself through which all the shrouds passed. This made a sensible pathway for a climber to gain the little platform that was the top, however no self-respecting topman would take that route.

Instead, by custom it was required to lean backwards high off the deck and clamber over the outside edge of the top. As captain, he could not possibly proceed on the easy path and face concealed ridicule from the hands. So he gritted his teeth and did it the proper way. Gaining the mizzen top, he felt a momentary glow of pride in himself, but then the hangover resumed its reminders.

Deciding then what he really wished was to get back down and rest in his bed, he reached out, clutched the mizzen's backstay and started to slide down. There was a trick to this that he had learned as a boy. One held on to the stay with one's hands, put the legs around the stay and start sliding, applying enough pressure to keep the descent at a moderate pace. However, over the years, he had lost the knack. Starting out initially sliding downward too fast, he attempted to slow himself by tightening his grasp. There was intense pain as the skin began stripping from his hands. In the end, he let gravity take its course as he rocketed downward. His left foot struck the deck first and he fell flat. When he attempted to rise, it was too painful. His foot and leg refused to function.

Someone passed the word for the doctor, and Baynes was there in a moment. Probing the area produced such pain that Phillips cried out and demanded he keep his hands to himself. Doctor Baynes reminded Phillips of the time when he had remonstrated with the doctor because Baynes did not respect his captain's authority. Now however, the shoe was on the other foot. It was Phillips who was not respecting Baynes authority in the medical field.

With poor grace, Phillips submitted and suffered the indignities. The doctor mixed up a physic that he compelled his patient to drink right down. The mixture was a concoction of the doctor's own invention and had both a horrible taste and a more terrible smell, but it did contain tincture of laudanum which soon put him to sleep.

181

When he wakened, he found his foot and leg had been bound with splints and much of the pain was gone. Even his hangover had dissipated. Baynes found he could avoid listening to his patient's bad temper by administering laudanum quite frequently. After being kept in a stupor for two days, the doctor permitted his patient to be carried on deck and installed in his deck chair.

Eventually, the two men discovered they had much to talk about. Phillips was able to explain to the bemused doctor the maze of rigging over their heads and how it was used to propel the ship in the direction required. In return, Baynes explained his ideas of how the human body functioned and how the humors controlled men's health.

By now, the doctor had reduced the massive doses of tincture of laudanum, and Phillips now had just a warm glow. His mental faculties were about normal, and he idly asked the doctor, "Do you remember during the dinner in the wardroom when we all had too much to drink? I have the recollection that we discussed where the pirate ship we are looking for might be based. Do you remember what we decided upon?"

The doctor thought. "As I recall, Lord Forsythe learned from the couple caring for him the pirate ship visited the Puerto Rico area quite often. I believe he said the ship even visited Vieques itself. In our inebriated state, we decided to look closely there."

As soon as Baynes uttered the words, Phillips recalled Forsythe mentioning something about pirates, but had not made the association with any particular lot.

This idea might be worth exploring more closely. He called Mister Hornady and asked him to consult with Mister Layton about a course back to Puerto Rico.

CHAPTER TWENTY FOUR

It was bitterly cold that evening. Master Commandant Elias Harrison of the United States Navy was in Parson Darby's church tower with his night glass observing the approaches to the harbor. There was a British frigate out there keeping a close watch on the port, with, who knew how many others waiting for unwary shipping to venture forth. Harrison's sloop, the USS Ethan Allen, had been towed last night out to an island in the outer harbor that screened her from view by the frigate's crew.

Parson Darby was something of a weather prophet. He and his father before him had kept careful records of the weather and Darby was famous for being able to predict the onset of bad weather long before it came. While the weather had been cold and clear earlier, now it was clouding over and it was Darby's prediction it would deteriorate by early morning with strong winds and snow.

Darby thought there would be a good chance the wind would be fair for leaving the harbor. It was just possible the snow might hide this departure from the eyes on the British frigate. If the prediction came to pass, Harrison aimed to take his sloop out to sea in the midst of the British blockade. He had his boat waiting at the waterfront now, to take him to the ship.

Darby pointed upwards as heavier cloud cover moved in, blocking out stars. The wind was picking up also. He spoke to the naval officer. "Elias, it is time you went to your ship. It may be a while before you get another chance."

His men were huddled under cloaks, taking turns to warm themselves beside a brazier burning on the dock. Bosun's Mate Harkins was in charge of the crew and reported them correct and mostly sober. Someone had produced rum which all had had a pull on to attempt to get some warmth in their bodies.

Leaving the brazier burning to amuse the lookout on the British frigate in the outer bay, they boarded the launch and made for the ship. It was a long pull, with visibility dropping constantly. By the time they reached it, they were depending on the boat compass to keep on course.

The Ethan Allen was a twenty gunned ship-sloop of the United States Navy. She had been tasked to get to sea and harry British commercial shipping sailing up the eastern coast. At the last minute, a letter from the Secretary of the Navy reported a pirate in the Caribbean area was preying on the few American commercial ships that had been able to get to sea. Harrison, in addition to attending to any British commerce he could intercept, was also charged to attend to the pirate.

It was not the economic trouble the pirate was causing that disturbed the Secretary. The British blockade was a much more serious factor there. It was the sheer savagery the pirates were inflicting upon innocent seamen and travelers that caused his ire.

185

Harrison was not quite sure what he could actually do about the pirate. It had been reported pirates had taken over a French frigate left behind on one of the former sugar islands when British troops took them from the French forces. The frigate had been moored in a creek mouth, and was unable to sail because of the lack of provisions and supplies. The crew attempted to burn her just as the British forces approached, but a sudden rain squall quenched the fire.

The British Infantry forces, with other matters on their mind, left the ship for their naval brothers to care for. Locals however, with an eye to the future, managed to get sail on her and somehow made it to an offshore island where she was hidden in a creek mouth that was camouflaged with vegetation.

As more locals became involved, some of the more corrupt among them became active and she soon became crewed by some very unpleasant pirates. The French had removed most of the ship's guns previously, but the pirates found a little powder and shot and used that with the few guns remaining to overawe a few trading ships when the frigate sailed out on short cruises. Using materials robbed from the cargoes of those ship, the frigate became more capable every week.

Originally, many of the crew were former peasants or ex-slaves with little knowledge of the sea, but soon some crewmen aboard captured merchants opted to join the pirates rather than fall victim to their little 'amusements'. Last month, an interesting addition to the crew had been found. The present captain and chief of the band had decided the hiding place for the ship was

186

becoming too well known, so it was decided to move the ship to another island.

A major problem was, nobody in the band could navigate properly. Sometimes fishermen among the crew were able to find their way around familiar waters just by studying the water's depth and the composition of the bottom. Outside their familiar area however, they were as helpless as any peasant.

It was necessary to move the ship frequently, so the British forces did not locate it. While the ship was being piloted gingerly to an island out of sight, they came across a small fore-and aft local sailing cutter ahead. Normally, they would not have wasted their time on such a worthless boat, but the captain thought he might learn from the boat crew exactly where they were. There was a surprise on this boat though. A British naval officer was aboard, trying to make Spanish Florida, he said. The pirate captain thought, surely there would be worth-while entertainment that night, perhaps the next also, if the victim did not expire too early.

While they were discussing his fate as well as the problems of navigating these waters, the naval officer, the runaway Lieutenant Granger, began to speak. He was fluent in French and knew a bit of Spanish also. He informed the captain he could navigate for them and eliminate all of this blundering around.

Captain Henri Poulain commander of the pirate crew was a mixed blood creole, He had gained his position among the pirates solely because of his ability to seize the opportunity and murder his opponents in an efficient and rapid manner. With not a smattering of any kind of education, he had assumed he could watch the English officer navigate and soon be able to do the same himself. This did not work out at all. With no understanding of mathematics, or even the ability to read or write there would be no hope of his becoming a navigator.

He had assumed he could have his hoped for entertainment later in the week after he had learned what he needed to know. Not a naturally stupid man, Poulain soon became aware of his limitations in the navigational field. After the ship was safely brought to safe harbor of the designated island, Poulain had a conference with Granger. It was acknowledged between them that Poulain would remain in actual command, but Granger would assume the position of that of a sailing master in a King's ship. Since no one else in the band had ever sailed in anything but a small fishing boat, it was becoming necessary for a skilled professional to handle the actual working of the ship. Accordingly, besides navigation, he would make sure the supplies on board were stowed in a safe manner, as well as seeing to the actual maintenance of the vessel. Perhaps he might train the crew into some semblance of professionalism.

He soon became a valued asset to the pirates and helped instill some training and discipline among the crew.

Granger soon showed the others how to pick their victims to gain the more useful spoils. From their prizes, they seized weapons and needed supplies. Soon, their gun ports, which had been mainly empty, were becoming filled as they seized guns from many of their prizes. Granted, the guns were of varying sizes and patterns, but they would serve the pirate ship's purpose. Many ship owners placed a few guns on their merchant ship, but then failed to provide the ammunition and training to the crews. The frigate 'Hortense' would not make this mistake.

Monsieur Poulain learned some interesting intelligence one night from a recent captive who was 'entertaining' them by his screams from the torture session. This person had been a Spanish officer assigned to an old fortress guarding a seldom used harbor on a neighboring island. When the pirates became active, the local authorities decided to staff the long abandoned fortress to offer protection to local vessels seeking refuge there.

Supplies and ammunition was shipped there and Señor Ortega was ordered to proceed to the island with his artillery troops and bring the fort to life. Unfortunately, Ortega's unit was one that had served for a lengthy period in the area and many of its senior ranks had died or retired. Ortega's predecessor had learned it was profitable to refrain from replacing those people. Simply by adding a fictitious name to the roster, he was able to put the pay for that invisible person into his own pocket. When Ortega assumed command, he followed the same practice, and it was a very small unit of artillery men that garrisoned the fort.

Poulain had learned from the nearly dead captive there was plenty of ammunition at the fort but few defenders. Guided there by former Royal Navy Lieutenant Granger, the ship arrived at the island in the dark of night, its crew travelling overland and storming into the sleeping installation at cock crow. The ammunition was seized, as well as some newly installed twelve pounder long guns that were on naval carriages. The ship remained a week, loading everything they wished and celebrating their good fortune.

In any event, Master Commandant Harrison had no need to worry about pirates just yet. The first order of business was to just get out of Boston Harbor. As the night wore on, the snow began to come. The westerly wind blew it almost horizontally, and both wind and snow increased as dawn neared. At last he could wait no longer. It was nearly blowing a blizzard now and he must leave. It was going to be a dangerous departure since he had no visual aids to depend upon. He was familiar with the harbor's bottom and had relay teams of leadsmen who would throw out the lead that would measure the water's depth as well as the type of bottom. With this information he would have some idea of the ship's position even when blinded by the weather.

At present they were moored behind the island that was hiding them from the enemy frigate. In addition, they had a cable out to an anchor to the north of the island. When Harrison judged the moment right, he ordered the cable slipped to their mooring and at the same time ordered the men at the capstan to start winding in the cable to the anchor.

At enormous effort, the ship was dragged away from its position behind the concealing island and out into the outer harbor. Away from the island, he was now ready to set sail. With the wind whipping at near hurricane strength, he feared to set too much canvas. He ordered just a scrap of fore staysail shown to the wind and a corner of canvas from the fore tops'l exposed. An axe man standing ready with his sharp blade, severed the anchor cable and USS Ethan Allen began scudding before the wind at an alarming rate.

Blinded by the blowing snow, it was necessary to have some means to determine just where in the harbor the ship might be.

The leadsmen were having difficulties. It was necessary to swing that lead weight far enough ahead to allow it to sink so the lead line was vertical in the water to allow the leadsman to read off the depth. And, it had to be done over and over again, constantly. Judging the bottom this way was the only means they had of determining their position in this weather.

With the frigid temperatures and the icy water from the lead line, the hands of the leadsmen became useless after only a few minutes. Exposed to the full force of the frigid wind and spray, their bare hands soon became numb and their fingers unable to distinguish the differing materials attached to the lead line every fathom. Without that touch, it would be easy to mistake a depth by a fathom or more. Men were brought up from below deck every half glass to take over the lead. Unfortunately, there were few trained leadsmen on board who could almost instinctively read off the depth of the sea.

It seemed they had been only under weigh a few minutes when they flashed by the silent, snow-covered outline of the British frigate. There was no indication she had seen them, and there would not have been time to respond anyway. The sun nominally came out shortly after leaving harbor, but there would be no sight of it today. The snow lasted until midmorning and by then they were out of sight of the blockading fleet and the shore. Lookouts were replaced every glass because of the frigid temperatures, especially for those aloft exposed to the full force of the wind. A humane captain might have brought them down in this weather, but their eyes were necessary to keep the ship and crew safe from patrolling blockade ships. Every ship she would spot would likely be a probably foe, and they must be spotted in time for the sloop to evade.

USS Ethen Allen sailed west until well out in the Gulf Stream where she patrolled for the enemy trade. Much of the commerce from the islands in the Caribbean came this way and the sloop of war was in the proper position to interfere. An order in council over in Britain had decreed all commercial shipping must sail in convoy, but that was not certain protection.

A week after venturing out, the lookout spotted a north-bound convoy. Dozens of ships of varying sizes in two columns, wending their way north toward Halifax. An old 64 gun line-of battle ship took the van, off the windward column. A brig of 16 guns was off the windward column in the center, and a sleek 32 gun frigate brought up the rear.

About the time the Ethen Allen's lookout spotted them, the signal flags began working on the escorts, so there would be no hope of surprise.

The American sloop of war took up station herself to windward of the convoy forward of the brig, almost as if she too was one of the escort. It soon became obvious that some of the cargo ship masters were now becoming nervous since there was much jockeying for position, and the flag signals were constantly busy. The escorts found it necessary to fire guns to enforce their commands, and Harrison was glad he was not one of those escort commanders.

The convoy seemed not to be as tight as it had been when it was first observed. Occasionally, he found it enjoyable to make a run at the convoy. Once he sailed right into the port column then came back through the scattering ships back out to windward again. There was not an opportunity to snatch up a quick prize, since he well knew the brig and then probably the frigate, would have been on him immediately had he done so.

This did not seem to disturb the escorts all that much, but many of the merchant ships would break formation to escape the perceived threat. This would have been stressful on some of them, since many masters sailed with depleted crews. Then again, it was not unknown for one of the escorting vessels to come alongside a merchant and press a few crew members. The result was, with insufficient crew aboard, some merchants had a difficult time with the added sail handling caused by the maneuvering.

All of this maneuvering gave Harrison's men some much needed drill at sail handling. As nightfall neared, he began informing his key people of his plans.

There was still heavy cloud cover and a rough sea when he made his move. With no starlight or moon, it was about as dark as it could be. Letting out some reefs, he began moving up the line of ships. His people could keep a fair idea of their position in relation to the convoy since most of the ships were showing some kind of light. Not so the Allen. His first officer had gone around the ship at dusk checking for light. Those people with tobacco were told to either chew it or throw it over the side. No smoking or lights of any kind were to be permitted.

At length, they were at the van. The big 64 gun liner was up there plodding along and some of the merchantmen had broken their column and clustered around her as if they were chicks huddling around the mother hen. Unseen, Allen eased over to starboard, closing a heavy looking brigantine as she labored along a few places astern of the battleship.

He was well aware he had little chance of successfully taking one of these ships as prize. In the first place, should he try, one or another of the escorts would be on him at once. Even if he did take one, and get it away from the convoy, he would never get it past the blockade. With his gunners having been ordered to fire high at the rigging, he came alongside and gave the target a broadside. The attack brought instant panic to the convoy. Merchant ships began breaking out of column and scattering in every direction.

Harrison took the opportunity to scatter himself. The massive 64 was coming around in her ponderous manner, and he wanted nothing to do with being a target for her big guns. Fortunately, the cluster of shipping around her precluded her from firing off her broadside.

In minutes, the sloop was racing away from the ships and was well out of reach of the blundering ship-of-the-line. Next morning, he saw the brigantine he had fired upon. She was lying broad to the swells, shrouds had been severed and her foremast was broken beneath the top. The brigantine was attempting to solve the problem with the few men she had aboard. Miles away, her absence had just been noted with the dawn, and the brig was rushing back to the rescue.

Captain Harrison was not in the least concerned about that brig. If he so desired, he knew he could fight her to a standstill, and make her his prize. That would be foolish though. The Royal Navy had dozens of escort brigs. The US Navy had only a few sloops and they were much too valuable to fritter away on ill-conceived individual actions. A fight between the two would likely leave both crippled to some extent. There would be an hour before the brig arrived so he sent the launch with an armed party over to the crippled vessel. They put the crew of the brigantine into her own boats and fired the prize. This would be one load of sugar which would never reach London. His crew was back aboard the sloop long before the brig arrived, and he took the time to dip his flag to her.

CHAPTER TWENTY FIVE

Phillips, although with a fair idea of where to look for the pirate now, knew it would still be a long search. The suspicion was she would be in one of her hiding holes in the innumerable bays and tiny harbors around Puerto Rico and the outlying islands. It could take quite a time before she was found, if she ever was. In the meantime, the larder was becoming low.

While there was still biscuit and pork, they were down to the bottom tier of casks of the salt beef. Occasionally, a bad cask was opened, and at this stage of the game, such a discovery could have unfortunate consequences. He decided this would be a good time to replenish his supplies. San Juan was just over the horizon, and while the Spanish government was often downright hostile to warships of other countries visiting their shores, the Regency government of Spain was, in fact, allied with Britain.

HMS Roebuck sailed into San Juan Bay and was greeted by a gun from the defensive fortifications. Phillips noted the seriousness with which the Spanish defenders took their entrance into the harbor, when an actual shot impacted the sea a cable's distance from them. The ship was immediately hove to at the warning and a boat bearing a white flag was launched. Lieutenant Wilson was permitted to land on shore and disappeared among a group of military officers waiting at the water's edge.

Later that day, Wilson returned to the boat and boarded Roebuck with a lengthy document he was to give to Phillips. A low-echelon clerk of the Spanish military service accompanied him to explain the various rules of the region and to translate for them.

Wilson had already made the preliminary arrangements while on shore and Phillips learned salt beef in casks would be brought out in barges to the ship at its mooring out in harbor. The ship herself would not be allowed to come closer to shore, but seamen, in small groups, would be permitted to go ashore, so long as they caused no trouble.

Well familiar with the ease a British seaman could get in trouble in a foreign port, Phillips decided then not to allow his people to leave the ship. Wilson had mentioned their hope to locate the pirate frigate that was causing so much trouble in the region and bring her in. The military commander with whom Wilson had discussed this with, was not un-responsive to the idea. That pirate ship 'Hortense' had caused plenty of financial trouble and misery all around the Caribbean.

Don Quevido, the local military commander however, was dubious of the ability of the British ship to take the pirate. He explained the rovers had been removing the guns from every ship they took, and now had quite an arsenal aboard the frigate. Also, they had somehow acquired a man to train and operate the ship in a more professional manner.

Quevedo greatly feared the pirates would overcome the small British warship easily enough, taking her into their service, and then the region would be confronted with a pair of pirate ships. The Spanish forces however would not prevent the Britons to do what they could against the pirates.

Taking aboard the needed supplies and water, even some additional powder purchased from the huge defensive fortress, Roebuck set out again.

She sailed up past Cuba and through the straits between that island and Florida. Phillips was tempted to sail northward up the mainland coast to Georgia or the Carolinas, with the object of taking a few Yankee merchantmen, but decided not to. At this stage of the war, few American ships were at sea and any that were afloat would likely be snatched up by one or another of the blockading fleet anyway. He sailed instead, east and south along the Atlantic coat of Cuba, looking into any bays or harbors he saw.

Phillips was not interested in the major ports, since the Spanish forces, naval and military, were just as angered by the piratical depredations as were the British, and would have surely noticed the presence of the pirate ship. However, the frigate could sail into some small bay or fishing port and compel the locals there to assist them. Too, they would need a place to dispose of the goods they had managed to take. With nothing remarkable noted, Roebuck continued her voyage. Near to the eastern end of the island, a small island schooner hove into sight one morning. It was a chance meeting. She had just put out from a small island offshore when Roebuck came along.

She let fly her sheets at the shouted command from the Spanish speaking crewman aboard the post ship, and came to a stop. Mister Richardson, a midshipman Phillips felt was coming right along, went over to her with his launch crew and the translator. After the examination, the lad bought a large turtle the schooner's crew had captured, and sent the relieved people on their way.

Phillips and Hornady went over to examine the enormous green turtle the lad had brought back to the ship. It was realized the beast was too large for the gunroom mess so Hornady bought it from the lad for the wardroom, with shares to go to the captain and the gunroom. With that important issue out of the way, Phillips asked Richardson what the schooner's crew had to say of their quarry.

The lad stated they had been chased by a big frigate two days earlier but had escaped by sailing closer to the wind than their pursuers were able. The crewmen of the small craft doubted it could be the pirate since all previous reports had it that the pirate was a shabby, run-down ship. This one showed signs of naval smartness, with her sails and rigging in good order and the ship handling what one might expect from a ship with perhaps a rather junior officer in charge of the deck.

Phillips decided this latter frigate might be from some other navy, scouting opportunities here in the tangled confusion of the Spanish territories.

Roebuck continued past Cuba back to Puerto Rico. This time paying close attention to the numerous islands. One fine Sunday morning found them anchored in a tiny bay on the lee side of a small island. It was a beautiful place with a fine beach and a thick forest behind the beach. It had been a lengthy period at sea and Phillips felt the men were becoming jaded. Accordingly, he gave instructions that port and starboard watches would be granted alternating liberty ashore.

Mister Hastings, their Marine officer would take a party of Marines ashore and examine the near jungle behind the beach for threats. Assuming no danger was evident, the first watch would proceed ashore while the watch on board would be vigilant for any danger.

Phillips accompanied Hastings ashore, taking along his rifle. Once past the beach, they entered the forest. It was difficult penetrating the thick jungle cover at first but they soon came to a clearing, halting when they heard the excited clatter of teeth from a group of pigs. Most were of small size, but one sow was probably close to 200 pounds.

The rifle was already loaded and at half cock. When that sow began looking as if she was about to attack, Phillips levelled the long rifle. She was less than fifty yards away, and could be a danger should she attack. Knowing his weapon would shoot a little high at this range, he placed the front bead on her upper neck and squeezed off the shot. Immediately, Hastings fired his musket at one of the smaller pigs and both animals dropped where they stood. The ball from Phillips' rifle took her in the mouth and entered her brain, killing her instantly.

The two officers stood by their kills while the corporal took the Marines on a quick scout to see if the shots had been noticed.

The corporal reported upon his return that he had seen no sign of another human being here. With this news, the pigs were dressed out and the carcasses carried out to the beach on poles. At the sight of the meat the liberty men on the beach immediately began building a fire and soon the smell of roasting pork filled the air.

After consuming a few slices of the fresh meat, Phillips returned to Roebuck and relieved Mister Layton. The first officer then began shuttling the men on the ship to the beach, bringing the sated members of the first watch back to the ship.

CHAPTER TWENTY SIX

Master Commandant Harrison stood by the windward rail of his quarterdeck with some difficulty. The sloop was pitching like a wild horse under him. Even after a lifetime at sea, his stomach was telling him it had nearly had enough. He had been exercising his mind for days, ever since he had first received these orders, studying just how he was going to carry them out.

Patrolling the seas off New England was not producing any results. Convoys were few and far between, and when they were found, produced few positive results, at least for his ship and the US Navy. He had not been able to duplicate the success of the attack on that first convoy soon after his escape from Boston. The shipping he did meet with all had capable, aggressive escorts.

Every day, looking over the reports from his department heads, he saw the consumable stores depleting steadily. Men were also being expended. Robert Jenson had been swept off the pitching deck by a rogue sea two nights ago. He went down immediately in the icy sea and was never seen again. Two men had been ruptured with the strenuous work required at sea and Ben Wilson had his foot crushed when the gun he was serving rolled over it. The surgeon doubted the foot could be saved.

He felt he was wasting his time now, but what else could he do? The blockade was strangling the ability of American ships to put to sea, naval and well as merchant. If he returned to port, there was no way to know if the ship could ever escape to sea again. As long as he was still out here, there must be some constructive action he could take.

The thought crossed his mind to cross the Atlantic, to take the battle to the enemy on his own shores. The problem was, he would be far from a friendly haven, and he had to expect his losses in men and stores were going to continue or even mount. Of course, he could always seek refuge in a French port, but he felt the blockade on those ports was probably as severe as was the one on the ports on the American coast. If he was to be blockaded, would it not be better to be home, rather than in a foreign country?

In the end, he decided to sail south, and at least make an effort to find that pirate the new Secretary of the Navy was upset with. He was almost certain he would not find a trace of the fellow or his ship, but at least they would be away from the cold weather. Too, there were all those British controlled islands with numerous ships sailing between them. Surely he could collect a few of them.

Having made up his mind, he called for his first officer. Mister Laird was a solemn Puritan, and not a joy to the fellow members of the wardroom, but he was a competent officer who was perfectly in tune with the ship. Phillips rather wished he was not so strict with the hands as to their language, but was willing to ignore his foibles and hoped the hands could learn to do so as well.

Mister Laird came up from below, with the expected sour look on his face. Harrison had planned on discussing the new plan with his second-in-command, but was put off by the man's expression and merely informed him he was going to his cabin to warm up a bit. He ordered Laird to put the ship on a course that would take them to the Caribbean. They were going pirate hunting.

Not wanting to go against the Gulf Current for the whole distance, Laird took them out to sea that day and turned south that evening. It was early in the morning watch when the officer of the watch sent down Jason Hendricks to wake him. Hendricks was a newly appointed midshipman of sixteen. He was not very knowledgeable about Navy affairs yet, but had served on his grandfather's merchant fleet for some years and had the makings of a seaman. "Sir", he shouted, "Mister Wilson says to tell you a ship is in sight."

Hendricks added, "I know her well, sir. She's the Amy Benson. She sailed out of Boston for years but now her owner Amos Hunter flies the British flag and sails out of Halifax."

Harrison grumbled, "Keep your voice down, Hendricks. I can hear you just fine."

Hendricks could not be satisfied unless he got the last word in. "Mister Wilson told me to make sure you were awake", using the same shout he had used before.

Groaning, Harrison donned his heavy wool coat and picked up the new bicorne hat his wife had given him before the voyage. Searching for his heavy gloves, he found them where his servant had hidden them away. Higgins thought they were much too fine and expensive to wear aboard ship, and was always hiding these items and leaving out his ancient, worn-out attire.

On the quarterdeck now, he shivered as the frigid wind found its way under his heavy coat. Although they had made some southing, it was just as cold here as it was to the north. His watch officer, Mister Wilson, approached and pointed out to starboard. "There sir, right on our beam."

A big, ship-rigged merchant was plodding along on her northerly course. Harrison wondered aloud, "I wonder what she is doing out here when she could be coming up the Gulf Stream, making port a little sooner?"

Young Hendricks was right there, shamelessly eavesdropping. "Sir, I know the man. Right now he flies the British flag on his ship so he can avoid the blockade. But he doesn't want to have to wait for convoys, so he sails out here where he thinks he will not be noticed."

"Won't the British fine him for not obeying that Order in Council?"

"No, that is the beauty of his plan. When he enters Halifax harbor, he hoists the American flag. Admiral Sawyer there is happy to have rogue American ships bring trade, so he says not a word about it. He will give a license to anybody that asks."

Harrison ordered the ship put about, and the Allen began coming up to the ship. It was high daylight before they came alongside, the ship ignoring their presence. When he fired a gun, the ship raised an American flag that matched their own, and kept sailing. The gunner tried another shot, and this clipped her cutwater, bringing forth some outraged gobbling from a portly gentleman on the merchant's deck.

Close enough now to use a speaking trumpet, Harrison shouted for the fellow to heave to. With no response, he warned, "Those last were warning shots, the next will go into your hull."

The remainder of the ports opened and the guns were rolled out. The merchant set her tops'ls to the mast and slowed to a crawl.

"Mister Laird", Harrison told the first officer. "I want you to take an armed party and examine that ship. Mister Hendricks will accompany you. He is to rummage the master's quarters, to see what he can find."

It was an hour before Laird returned to the sloop with a case full of papers. Young Hendricks had remained on the merchant with some armed hands. Laird approached his captain and announced. "When I went aboard that merchant, her master handed me her papers and manifest. Supposedly, she is the Amy Benson whose home port is Boston. She has a cargo of tobacco from Virginia in hogsheads bound for Boston, or Halifax, depending on which set of papers you want to believe."

"When we went past her stern before boarding, the sternboard said she was the Amy Benson out of Halifax, but she has another sternboard under that one saying she is out of Boston."

"Young Hendricks worked as an apprentice for that master two years, and knows some of his little tricks. He found one set of documents in the cabin saying she was a British ship and another proving she was American. Amos Hunter, her owner and master, has papers identifying himself as an American and as an Englishman. Apparently Mister Hunter wishes to be all things to all people."

Harrison had himself pulled over to observe matters himself. The master of the ship was most indignant of his treatment and would surely call upon the new Navy Secretary, Mister Jones, and forcefully express his displeasure.

Leaving the master in the hands of his Marines, Harrison had a hatch opened. Hogshead after hogshead was wedged tightly in place. He approached his bosun's mate standing by the hatch and asked if he could knock in the top of one of the large oaken casks. He wanted to see the contents.

Obligingly the seaman located an axe and had a top knocked in within a few minutes. The pungent aroma of Virginia tobacco emerged. "Dayton, I am planning to burn this ship. If you or your mates wish any of this tobacco, and have a place to stow it, you may take what you will."

Harrison had it in mind that every tobacco user aboard ship would take a few pounds of tobacco from the huge barrel. After returning to the Ethan Allen, he looked out his stern window and saw the Benson's windlass cranking a hogshead through the open hatch from the end of a cable leading through a block on the mainyard. As he watched, his crew braced the yard around until the container hung over the side. The Benson had a big barge on board and that had been dropped into the sea and led under the hanging hogshead. Slowly, the barrel was lowered into the barge, making it settle deeply into the water from the half ton weight of the tobacco.

How they were going to stow it on the Ethan Allen, he had no idea and knew better than to ask.

The first tendrils of smoke began seeping through the open hatches before they set sail. Soon after, flames began gushing out and she was then fully engulfed. Harrison had sacrificed a jug of whale oil that he had intended to use for his lamps on the voyage. He decided he could just use slush from the galley instead.

Mister Hunter was confined to a little storeroom the bosun said they could use. He had a stool to sit on and the deck on which to sleep. A bucket for his bodily wastes, which he could empty over the side once a day and a Bible, although he would have a difficult time reading it for lack of a lamp. When he complained bitterly, he was told he could sleep in irons on the orlop deck if he preferred.

The USS Ethan Allen continued south, once sighting a dozen ships heading in their own direction. Closing to inspect them, they found three of them were British warships, two frigates and a ship-sloop. Wanting to say nothing to any of them, Allen hoisted everything she could carry and the race was on. The big 38 gun frigate was soon sunk under the horizon, but the sloop and the smaller frigate were not so easily left behind. The pair remained with the American ship the rest of the day, the Allen escaping only in the dark of night. Harrison would have gladly met with the ship-sloop by herself, but an action would have only bad results if the frigate was present too.

Harrison was becoming depressed. He commanded a warship and his duty was to seek out and destroy any enemy warships he met. Here he was, slinking around like a burglar, hiding from everyone, almost afraid to come out in the open.

The men though, seemed to be taking it in stride. They were in the warmer waters of the south and men were now caulking on deck on their off watches, taking the sun and working on scrimshaw.

One day, while taking noon sights with the midshipmen, he found they had left Florida, the last appendage of the North American mainland in these parts and were closing Cuba. He had no instructions concerning these Spanish areas. While Spain was technically an ally of Britain in her was with France, he knew of no reason why the United States should not be at amity with Spain.

He decided it might be worthwhile to send a boat into San Juan harbor to find if he could bring the Ethan Allen into the port to load supplies and find out more of this pirate ship. It had been months since Navy Secretary William Jones had issued the orders for this mission. The pirate could well have been taken long since and his bones might be decorating some gibbet along the shore somewhere,

Harrison selected Mister Laird to take the boat in. Although he was not the most pleasant person to deal with, he had a good head on his shoulders and was able to make clear decisions rapidly. Laird was dead-set against 'Papists' and was apt to fly into a rage discussing them. Harrison reminded him the people in these parts were Roman Catholics, and he must not discuss religion with them.

It was nightfall when the boat returned. Laird had had a productive day on shore. Their quarry was still terrorizing the local populace and the American's efforts to suppress this menace were welcome. Supplies were available but it was not deemed advisable for crew to come ashore on liberty. A pilot would come out in the morning to take them to their anchorage.

CHAPTER TWENTY SEVEN

The men of the Roebuck were in a better frame of mind after their liberty away from the ship. They found a creek which they used to fill the few empty water barrels and set sail again. Thinking back, Phillips thought he remembered Lord Forsythe mentioning his caregivers telling him of the pirates sometimes frequenting Viequez. Even if they did not make the island a permanent base, it might be worthwhile to make exploratory visits now and then.

Their minds and bodies refreshed, the crew of Roebuck set sail again. Still sailing along the Puerto Rican coastline, they tried to inspect every small bay and inlet they came to. Their interpreter learned a few inhabitants had seen a big frigate, but whether it was the pirate, nobody knew.

Approaching San Juan harbor, Phillips decided to enter and learn of any news before going on to inspect Viequez.

Having already visited the port before, Phillips was ready this time and the fortress did not find it necessary to fire a warning shot. They hoisted the signal for a pilot who came to them as soon as he had delivered his previous ship to her mooring.

As they were ghosting through the quiet harbor to the anchorage, Phillips spotted a trim little sloop-of-war

211

flying the American flag. After the port doctor came aboard to listen to Phillips oath that no man had suffered any contagious disease recently, they were granted practique. Certain officers, including the ship's doctor, were permitted to go ashore to make necessary arrangements. The doctor needed to purchase certain medicaments, as well as some green foods for the relief of health problems among the men. The purser had his own purchases to make. The men's tobacco supply was getting low and this was a good port to purchase rum.

Phillips went ashore with the ostensible purpose to meet with Don Quevido again. The official was indeed free and met with him in front of a posada by a nearby plaza. Warning Phillips he himself had a meeting scheduled with the archbishop that very morning, they had a short discussion where it was soon found that neither had any new information. The pirate frigate was still continuing its depredations and it was still not known where it might be based. There were a thousand islands where it could be and the corsairs could be using several or many of them alternatively. Quevido left for his appointment and Phillips sat there at the little table wondering how he was to spend the time ashore. While he was debating himself, he noticed a uniformed man settling in at another table.

When the stranger shifted his sword to a more comfortable position and removed his hat, he paid more attention. During his service in the Mediterranean, Phillips had met several American Naval officers, and this one was wearing the uniform. He must be from that American warship in the harbor.

With most of a bottle of wine in his belly, Phillips began thinking of his options. This was an officer of a nation with which his country was at war. But, he was in a neutral country where it would be folly to go forth, waving his sword. He could just sit here and ignore the fellow. Or, he could saunter over and introduce himself. Of course, neither could discuss their missions or plans, but they were officers of respectable services. Surely a little courtesy could not be amiss?

A waiter came by then and asked an undecipherable question in Spanish. He did not understand the language but when the lad pointed to his empty bottle, Phillips nodded and put a coin on the table. A new, opened bottle was promptly placed before him. Picking up the bottle and his glass, he went over to the stranger's table and looked questioningly at the empty chair.

The American officer had obviously been observing him also and waved him to the empty seat with a grin. "Master Commandant Harrison of the USS Ethan Allen, sloop-of-war". He said. You are with that British sloop anchored near me."

"Well", answered Phillips, "Since I'm actually a post captain, she has to be a post ship."

"Yes, Your Majesty", offered Harrison, knuckling his forehead like a seaman approaching a senior officer."

"That's alright, Master Commandant. I just did not want you to get the idea my ship was a mere sloop."

The waiter had brought a glass and placed it before Harrison, so Phillips filled it with wine. Wordlessly, the two officers sat and meditated the subjects they were to discuss with each other.

It was Phillips who brought up the subject of the pirate. Surely that would not conflict with his duty.

Harrison responded. "It is curious that you mention that, Captain. My Secretary of War dispatched me down here to see what I could do about the fellow. It seems Secretary Jones is upset over the un-necessary barbarities the pirates are inflicting on their captives."

Phillips nodded. "I have been chasing him for weeks now. I can't seem to pin him down. But, I have intelligence he is using haunts around Puerto Rico, One said he was using a base on the Isla Vieques, off to the east of Puerto Rico recently."

"Then, you should be thanking your lucky starts you have not found him. That frigate has some serious armament aboard his ship!"

"Oh, as a King's ship, we are expected to go up against serious opposition. And this pirate, even though he is sailing in an old French 40 gun frigate, is not quite up to the standard of her former owners, the professional French Navy. Most of those guns were missing when the ship began its new career. It has been re-armed with whatever could be gleaned from its merchant prizes, probably four and six pounders."

Nodding, Harrison answered. "I think that was true originally. However I spoke a Spanish Garda Costa vessel early yesterday and learned the pirates had sacked an old Spanish fortress near here. The fort was nearly abandoned but the pirates got the guns, twelve pounders, all on naval carriages. They also seized a large supply of ammunition that had just been delivered. I think either of us encountering the frigate will have a fight on our hands!"

With plenty to think about, Phillips returned to the ship.

Early in the morning watch the next day, he was wakened by the midshipman of the watch. "Sir, a boat from that Yankee sloop is alongside with a message."

"Well, have them hand the damned thing up!"

"Shall we allow them to board?"

"No, we will not. We are combatants, for God's sake!"

When Phillips had shrugged into his uniform coat and placed his hat on his head, he emerged onto the quarterdeck. The officer of the deck nervously presented him with a sealed document. Phillips ripped the thing open ungraciously.

It was from Master Commandant Harrison, expressing his interest in the subject of their *tête-a tête* ashore yesterday. If the captain of HMS Roebuck were interested, he would like to propose further discussion of that topic, only at a place of Captain Phillips choosing.

Phillips needed to think this over carefully. Discussions with an enemy combatant could easily lead him into shoal waters. It was only after he read over his orders advising him of the importance of dealing with this pirate that Phillips decided to gingerly approach the subject with this American captain.

A brief visit to the British Consulate brought additional news that gave him thought. He needed to discuss this news with another person of like mind as himself.

Accordingly, for the sake of secrecy, he sat down without the aid of his clerk, who had a better hand with a pen than himself and penned a letter to Master Commandant Harrison advising him that he must be very circumspect about approaching any level of co-operation between the two warships, but expressed his interest in re-visiting the subject at the same establishment they had met before at the same time of day.

Addressing the note to Master Commandant Harrison, USS Ethan Allen, and sealing it, he impressed his personal seal into the wax and called for his coxswain.

Cox'n Mullins, as Phillips knew from the 'X' he had signed the muster book, was perfectly illiterate, although an excellent seaman for all that. Taking Mullins out on deck, he looked out at the American warship.

"Mullins, I have a task for you which I hope you can perform without it being discussed on the mess deck. I wish you to deliver this note to that American warship, and hand it up to her anchor watch officer. There will be no reply. There will be no banter between your boat's crew and people aboard the American. Our countries are at war, as you know, so we must be discreet. Do you understand?"

"Sir, I didn't understand some of the words you used, but I will deliver the note, and the boat's crew will keep their mouths shut."

"There you have it, Mullins. Take care of it at once, if you please."

CHAPTER TWENTY EIGHT

Harrison was waiting at the posada when Phillips arrived. They each ordered a bottle of wine and cigars from the waiter. A lamp was placed on the table with the drink and tobacco, and the waiter trimmed the cigars for them.

"Well", began Harrison. "What are we to discuss?"

"Just this! Both of us must be circumspect if we do not want to bring down the wrath of our respective governments upon our heads. In my own case, my instructions are to do what I can to eliminate this pirate. I assume you have similar instructions. From the intelligence you gave me yesterday, it seems this fellow may be a tough nut to crack, by either one of our warships. I have a little added intelligence that I have since learned from our consul here."

"A British officer, a former lieutenant of the Royal Navy, Mister Granger, has deserted his post to avoid probable court martial proceedings. It is suspected he has joined this pirate, a Monsieur Henri Poulain, aboard the old French frigate, 'Hortense'. From the reports of the few survivors, the Hortense has seemingly became more capable in recent months, and it is thought this Granger has begun training his people to the standards of the Royal Navy. I feel he has probably not been able to bring them along that far, but they could still be a formidable enemy."

"Should either of us engage that enemy on our own, there is the probability that either ship will become so battered that it may well be in-effective."

"My government, furthermore, will be very upset with me if I were to enter into any alliance with you against this pirate. At best, I could expect to be drummed out of the Royal Navy. The worst, I would not like to think about."

Harrison, having now fired up his smoke satisfactorily, wondered, "Just where are you going with this, Phillips? It looks like you think this will be an impossible situation."

"Not at all, Harrison. I believe there may be a place where our enemy is based, on the Isla Vieques off the end of Puerto Rico. I am not sure exactly where on that island he may be, but I do think it well worth searching. I propose to leave tomorrow, as early as the wind and tide permit. I will proceed directly to the island and begin my search."

"Of course, as a Royal Naval officer, I am unable to enter into any alliance with you as to actions to be taken, but I will say, should you happen to stumble upon a battle between myself and the pirate, I would be unlikely to protest, if you happen to join in. Should we, independently, bring this pirate to action, I myself, will not mention in my log any assistance you might give."

Harrison took a drink from his glass, then attempted unsuccessfully to blow a smoke ring. "I can never do this properly," he grumbled. He then wondered, "The Spanish probably won't let me follow you right out. They will think we will go at it hammer and tongs in their territorial waters."

Phillips thought a bit. "My sailmaker bought some good canvas here in San Juan. My fore mast staysail is becoming thin, and we have to think of hurricanes come spring."

"If the weather permits, I may take my time sailing around Puerto Rico to allow a new staysail to be made up. They may have to send it up a few times before it is correct. Even if you left a day after myself, you could probably still find me easily enough."

The morning breeze wafted Roebuck from San Juan Harbor. USS Ethan Allen, immediately slipped her mooring and set out after her, only to have the harbor Guarda Costa gunboat pull up and fire a gun.

The American warship could have easily blown the fragile gunboat from the water, but the guns of the harbor defenses were loaded and trained. Any offensive action would bring a swift reply. Accordingly, Allen went back to her mooring accompanied by the Guarda Costa. The gunboat's commander smiling incomprehensively at Harrison's threats and sputtering.

After picking up her mooring, Harrison after some reflection, ordered Mister Hunter brought up from below. He had long since been released from his shackles, and had been set to work performing menial chores for the senior petty officers of the crew.

Harrison gave him a little talk about the danger he was in, trading with the enemy, and assured the former ship-owner he would leave his name and past smuggling activities with the American consul. He reminded the man the American government could have a long memory and he would be well advised to do his business elsewhere in the future. The fellow was then bundled into a bum-boat and set free. With no funds, alone in a Spanish seaport, it would be a long time before the fellow could get back into the smuggling business up north.

Roebuck's lookout spotted the island early in the forenoon watch and hands were sent to stations. They had been searching for their quarry for weeks now, and no one really expected to sight the frigate. It was with some surprise, with Roebuck sailing by the entrance of the very bay they had entered weeks ago to rescue Lord Forsythe, a boat was seen in the process of emerging from the heavily overgrown mangroves concealing the entrance.

Phillips had no real reason to believe this boat was not just some innocent fishermen trying their luck and he put back out to sea. Hove to, a mile offshore, the crew waited to see what would emerge from the dense foliage. The boat had gone back inside, but now, here she was again, accompanied by three more. One appeared to be a scout and came out under sail, while the other three were towing something at the end of heavy cables.

The scout, a standard ship's launch under sail, approached within easy viewing distance, then put about instantly and went back to the others. The towing boats, with some effort, pulled a heavy frigate slowly from its refuge. Stopping long enough to put its people back on board, the frigate took her boats in tow and set sail. Phillips was taken aback when he saw the behemoth. She was one of the ubiquitous French-built frigates, of which the Royal Navy had taken a few in battle.

This one had been modified by the addition of new gun ports haphazardly cut into the ship's side. These guns were now being run out and there were more than two dozen of them protruding from the frigate's gun ports of the side facing HMS Roebuck.

Looking carefully through his glass, he could see there were an interesting variety of weapons, but many of them appeared to be of about twelve pounder caliber. One of those guns spouted smoke and fire and a worrisome sized splash lifted a column of water. That was no twelve pounder. More like a thirty two!

Mister Hornady was beside him on the quarterdeck. He observed, "It looks to me he has overloaded himself with guns. I wonder that she has not warped her keel."

Phillips looked carefully through his glass. "She doesn't look hogged to me Mister Hornady, although I think you are right. She could well find herself in trouble soon. For now, though, we are the ones who could find ourselves in trouble with all of those guns she has."

Hornady offered, "It's too bad the Americans can't take part in this fight too. It would be in their interest."

"I don't see how, Mister Hornady. We have just about ruined their Caribbean trade, so the pirates can't be harming them all that much. And, you will note, we are at war with the Americans."

The big frigate was now under sail and moving right along. Phillips wished to see just how she sailed, compared with Roebuck. It soon looked as though the heavy frigate was having difficulty with all the weight she had aboard, much of it on her upper deck. It seemed there would be no difficulty in staying out of her clutches, but the question was, how the devil were they to damage that huge frigate?

Roebuck was sailing easterly, with the trade wind on their port quarter, Hortense following to port a bit, abaft their stern. Having gained a bit, Phillips told Mister Layton, the sailing master to wear ship and put her across the frigate's bow.

Coming on her new course, about south-west, her starboard battery was aimed directly at Hortense. The frigate was heading for them as Roebuck crossed her bow, but her commander probably did not fancy being raked by the post ship's starboard battery, so she tried to tack. Unfortunately, tacking was a skill the frigate's officer of the deck, a former cane cutter in the fields of his home island, had not quite mastered yet.

Mister Granger was at the guns of the big pirate, planning to match broadside with broadside when his ship came around. Unfortunately, the ship missed stays, and she lay there, unable to get around. The big ship was right in position to receive the broadside of Roebuck, and there were more than a few of the crew that wished they were back in the comparative safety of those cane fields right then.

The fusillade of heavy balls ripped the length of the pirate ship maiming men and dismounting guns. Unfortunately for the British ship, no important rigging or spars were damaged.

Granger ran to the quarterdeck and got the ship back to the wind again and under control, when he was able to tack successfully, this time. Both ships turned to the northwest, Hortense inside the Roebuck now, and just within range of her portside guns. They raced along, Hortense pacing Roebuck for a bit, until she began falling behind again.

CHAPTER TWENTY NINE

Some of the pirate's shot came aboard Roebuck as the pair ran along. None injured her masts or rigging, but men were wounded and equipment damaged. The post ship fired in reply, but no hits were observed. It was then the maintop lookout reported the Yankee ship coming at them from ahead.

Mister Hornady, not knowing of the plans, was concerned. "I wonder who she is going to engage when she nears."

"Make sure the gunners know our target remains the frigate. No one will fire on the American until she fires at us, or I order it so."

Hornady wanted to discuss their plans for the American and was reluctant to go onto another subject. "She could stay out of range until both the frigate and we are crippled, then come in and finish us both off."

A pair of twelve pound shot coming through the rail killed a sail handler and caused several gun crew to be quilled by oak splinters. This caused the first officer to devote his attention to the ship, a job he should have been doing in the first place, in Phillips view.

The gunfire was continuous now, but it certainly looked as if Roebuck was firing faster than Hortense. Phillips noted that some individual guns of the frigate were firing at half the rate as those of Roebuck. They were pulling ahead again, but now some of the forward guns were having trouble slewing around to fire effectively at the frigate.

The American was approaching, USS Ethan Allen was closing to starboard of the frigate, as if she was planning on exchanging broadsides. Before reaching the frigate, she changed her mind and veered, turning across the bows and firing her broadside down the length of the pirate's hull. The American had only twelve pounder guns, and it took many hits to seriously degrade the enemy, but the pirate was now receiving those hits from both of her opponents. Deciding to finish this some other day, she tried to come about with the intention of fleeing.

The Allen continued down the lee side of the ship, where surprisingly, the guns seemed to be poorly manned. While the Allen was pouring her twelve pound balls and grape into the frigates hull, Roebuck found herself on the frigate's quarter, and she was able to slam in her shot without much in the way of a reply.

Now, the frigate's rudder was smashed and she was unable to come about. Allen wore around and made her way back to the frigate's bow, and went back to work there without the bother of receiving much attention herself.

Soon, both ships were just engaging in target practice, one mast after another came down aboard the pirate ship. Hortense merely firing single shots now and again. Hornady wondered why she did not yield, but Phillips had the time now to tell him that those on board the ship knew well it was the high jump for all of them, so they might as well go down fighting.

Hortense was dead in the water, having lost her masts as well as the rudder. She had countless openings smashed in her hull, and now it was fire also. Her guns stopped firing as those crewmen still capable appeared on deck to escape the smoke that was starting to billow from the hatches. A few of the pirates that could swim leaped overboard.

A mild 'whump' sounded, and a section the foredeck was blown upward, then a resounding explosion as fire reached her magazine. Her upperworks were blown skyward, some of the debris afire. Material of all sorts were falling on the two surviving ships. Aboard Roebuck, the emphasis now was on fighting fire rather than firing the guns. Ethan Allen was in a better condition, since she had been slightly farther away than Roebuck had been.

Falling debris, some aflame, had set some of Roebuck's sails smoldering and the fore topsail was actually aflame. All hands were busy for an hour, dousing smoldering brands with seawater, and wetting down the remaining sails. Fortunately, she had entered the engagement under topsails alone, and when these had been secured, the ship seemed safe enough.

A problem occupied Phillips while his people fought the flames. Ethan Allen was able to extinguish her minor fires early on. While she looked singed and scorched, when she got her spare canvas aloft, she looked ready for another action. Granted, she was much battered with some empty gun ports, but she still seemed capable for another engagement.

Not so with Roebuck. Her main mast was only standing because of the few intact shrouds and stays still holding it up. At the moment, it would not hold a press of sail. Her pumps were expelling tons of water up to the deck, where it ran into the scuppers and then overboard. He had lost dozens of men, killed and wounded, and those still on their feet were exhausted, with much work still to be done, if Roebuck was to stay on top of the waves.

Harrison, he knew, had behaved honorably during the engagement with the pirate, but now he had every right and duty to attack his enemy, HMS Roebuck.

At the moment, the British post ship could not maneuver. Much of the rigging, damaged by fire, must be re-rove and sails brought up from the sail locker. He must get that mainmast fished so that it would stand up under sail. Phillips, at that moment, almost despaired. He could not imagine how he was to make the necessary repairs as well as fight another action. Just staying afloat would require every bit of energy his people had.

Lost in his thoughts, he was caught by surprise when he saw his men pointing. USS Ethan Allen had set all plain sail, and was now beating into the north-westerly wind on the port tack. As she steadied on her course, her flag was seen to dip.

Phillips turned to the first officer. "Hurry, Mister Hornady, get somebody to dip our ensign."

Hornady protested, wondering as to the propriety of saluting an enemy. Phillips asked him quietly if he would rather open fire on the American while she was still in range.

It was in early winter when they reached the latitude of Boston. They were into the last of the casks of that Spanish beef they had taken aboard all those months ago. Phillips wondered if Harrison was still at sea, or if he had managed to get by the blockade into one of the American ports. He himself would be glad to sail into Halifax soon. He wondered what Admiral Sawyer would have to say after reading his reports. As he saw it, the only positive aspect to his cruise was the victory over the pirate ship, and that American sloop had as much to do with the outcome as the Roebuck.

Phillips had now a good understanding why his father had taken a temporary retirement from the sea. He had not wished to fight his American friends, and now the son was of the same opinion.

EPILOGUE

Granger, still aboard Hortense, saw the end coming. Fire had broken out below and the crew was so decimated there were not enough people to fight it, even if they were willing to obey orders. Most were not. Terrified men scrambling about, attempting to find a safe hiding place or to gather some of the wealth that had accumulated on the ship in recent months. Few men were still fighting.

From his place at the taffrail, Granger saw a boat still towing behind. This had been one of those used to pull the ship from its hiding place on Vieques. The others had been shattered, but this one was still partially afloat. Seeing a few pirates throwing themselves overboard, Granger had a thought. There were sharks in the water, but they did not seem especially active at the moment. A twelve pound shot passing inches away from his body, decided him. He had been one of the rare members of the Royal Navy who could swim.

Now, he threw himself overboard and began stroking for that boat. Reaching up, he was able to undo the painter that was connecting the boat to the wreck of the frigate. Drifting free, he hid himself among some other trash alongside the boat.

The explosions aboard Hortense did not cause any significant problems to him. Although a large amount of smoldering wreckage was blasted aloft, no major parts of the ship landed near him. In due course, a boat from the English ship came over to inspect the half-swamped launch, but found it empty, with a large shot hole in her side. The midshipman in charge of Roebuck's boat judged the craft worthless and left it for the currents to dispose of. The boat left, as did the ship shortly after.

With some effort, Granger was able to scramble into the boat and see what he had to work with. Using floating sailcloth and wreckage floating nearby, he was able to put a temporary patch over the shot hole. The boat still had some of its tools aboard, including its bailer and the mast and sail.

After a great deal of effort, he was able to get most of the water out, and to set sail. He had no food or water aboard, but the island was only a half dozen miles away, and there, at the old camp site, was all the water he could drink, plus an emergency cache of food, weapons and supplies the pirates had left for possible use later.

It was dark when the boat made its way to the access channel to the hidden bay. Granger was confident. He knew he would survive this little episode.

Made in the USA
San Bernardino, CA
13 August 2015